# ARE YOU DEPRESSED?

# ARE YOU DEPRESSED?

Don Rauf and
Eileen Lucas

SADNESS
OVERWHELMED
LONELINESS
NO CONTROL
EMPTINESS
HOPELESSNESS

Enslow Publishing
101 W. 23rd Street
Suite 240
New York, NY 10011
USA
enslow.com

Published in 2016 by Enslow Publishing, LLC.
101 W. 23rd Street, Suite 240, New York, NY 10011

Copyright © 2016 by Eileen Lucas

Publishing materials copyright © 2016 by Enslow Publishing, LLC.

All rights reserved.

No part of this book may be reproduced by any means without the written permission of the publisher.

**Cataloging-in-Publication Data**
Rauf, Don.
 Are you depressed? / by Don Rauf and Eileen Lucas.
    p. cm. — (Got issues?)
 Includes bibliographical references and index.
 ISBN 978-0-7660-6981-7 (library binding)
  1. Depression, Mental — Juvenile literature. 2. Depression (Psychology) — Juvenile literature. I. Rauf, Don. II. Title.
 RC537.R38 2016
 616.85'27— d23

Printed in the United States of America

**To Our Readers:** We have done our best to make sure all Web sites in this book were active and appropriate when we went to press. However, the author and the publisher have no control over and assume no liability for the material available on those Web sites or on any Web sites they may link to. Any comments or suggestions can be sent by e-mail to customerservice@enslow.com.

Portions of this book originally appeared in the book *More Than the Blues? Understanding and Dealing With Depression*

**Disclaimer:** For many of the images in this book, the people photographed are models. The depictions do not imply actual situations or events

**Photo Credits:** Alexander Kalina/Shutterstock.com, p. 106; Antonio Guilem/Shuttestock.com, p. 20; Bob Rosato/Sports Illustrated/Getty Images, p. 13 (Ricky Williams); Christy Thompson/Shutterstock.com, p. 35; David Smart/Shutterstock.com, p 51; Evgeny Atamanenko/Shutterstock.com, p. 7; Everett Collection/Shutterstock.com, p. 12 ( Janet Jackson); Executive Office of the president of the United States/wikimedia/public domain ( J.K. Rowling), p. 12; Iakov Filimonov/Shutterstock.com, p. 95; iatlo/Shutterstock.com, p. 83; Jaren Jai Wicklund/Shutterstock.com, p. 25; joesayhello/Shutterstock.com, p. 63; Jupiterimages/Photos.com/Thinkstock, p. 79; Kamira/Shutterstock.com, p. 40; Kuttelvaserova Stuchelova/Shutterstock.com, p. 46; Library of Congress Prints & Photographs Division/wikimedia/public domain, p. 13 (Abraham Lincoln); Micahelpuch/Shutterstock.com, p. 53; MIGUEL GARCIA SAAVEDREA/Shutterstock.com, p. 102; Mr. Tobin/Shutterstock.com, p. 90; NASA photo, p. 13 (Buzz Aldrin); nobeastsofierce/Shutterstock.com, p. 37; parinyabinsuk/Shutterstock.com, p. 43; Piotr Marcinski/Shutterstock.com, p. 3; Radharani/Shutterstock.com, p. 31; Robert Kneschke/Shutterstock.com, p. 93; Samuel Borges Photography/Shutterstock.com, p. 27; s_buckly/Shutterstock.com, p. 12 ( Jim Carrey), p. 13 (Amanda Beard); Sarah2/Shutterstock.com, p. 74; Suchota/Shutterstock.com, p. 17; Suzanne Tucker/Shutterstock.com, p. 15; toxipedia.org/Creative Commons Attrbution, p. 59; Twin Design/Shutterstock.com, p. 45; vesna cvorovic/Shutterstock.com, p. 66; wavebreakmedia/Shutterstock.com, pp. 69, 71; Zsschreiner/Shutterstock.com, p. 33.

**Cover Credit:** Piotr Marcinski/Shutterstock.com (depressed teen).

# Contents

**Chapter 1** Into the Bleak ........................7

**Chapter 2** Recognizing the Signs ................20

**Chapter 3** The Root of the Blues ................33

**Chapter 4** A Prescription for Depression........51

**Chapter 5** Mental Therapy and Beyond .........69

**Chapter 6** Conditions Related to Depression....83

**Chapter 7** Getting Help........................93

Chapter Notes .....................109

Glossary..........................119

For More Information .............122

Further Reading ..................123

Index.............................125

# Into the Bleak

In 2011, Kevin Breel was a popular seventeen-year-old in high school. He had a lot of friends. He was captain of his school basketball team. He'd walk through the school smiling, laughing, and high-fiving people. He was the drama student of the year. He was English student of the year. He always made honor roll. He showed up at all the parties. Family, friends, and classmates thought he was a happy student.

But Kevin said he was putting on an act. Inside, he just couldn't feel happy. A best friend of his had died in a car crash, and his parents had divorced. These events may have set off a deep feeling of sadness in him. Kevin poured a lot of his energy into sports to try to wipe out these feelings. But even after winning a major high school basketball tournament, he couldn't free himself of the anguish. Kevin said that even when everything in his life was going right, he was feeling down.

One night he took a bottle of pills, a pen, and some paper and went to his bedroom. He sat on the edge of his bed and thought about taking his life. As he started to write down his thoughts, he realized he had never told anyone about his problem. He had never reached out to a parent, coach, teacher, or friend to get help. He thought to himself that he wouldn't give up on himself until he tried to help himself.

Kevin thought that there was so much stigma about depression that he had held it in and hid it from all. In a speech he gave about his battle with depression, Kevin said, "We live in a world where you break your arm and everyone runs over to sign your cast. But if you tell people you're depressed, everyone runs the other way." He wanted to tell people that if you're depressed, you're not weak, you're sick. At age nineteen, Kevin gave a TED (Technology, Entertainment, Design) talk on the subject and encouraged people to get over the mark of disgrace associate with depression and get the help they need—just as he has done. Kevin says he still lived with depression, but he now has gotten the help he needs to continue forward and help others.[1]

## Defining Depression

This is one young man's story. There are countless others. They vary in their details. And this mood disorder can affect almost anyone regardless of sex, race, age, or income. It can affect those who seem to have everything going for them. Those who have money, fame, and the love of family and friends can still be brought low by depression. In 2014, the comedian Robin Williams lost his battle with depression and took his own life.[2]

As each individual is different, so is the experience of depression, but there are some common threads. Depression comes in many shapes and sizes and occurs more often than many people think. In fact, it is said to be the most common mental health disorder. It is so prevalent that it has been called the common cold of mental illness. Nearly everyone suffers from it to some degree at sometime in his or her life.

*Into the Bleak*

In 2012, an estimated sixteen million adults had at least one major depressive episode during the past year, according to the National Institute of Mental Health. That number is about 7 percent of all US adults.[3] The Centers for Disease Control and Prevention says that in any given year close to nineteen million Americans suffer from a depressive illness. Some say the number of people reported with depression is far fewer than the number who really have the illness. A large percentage of Americans are thought to have it, but it often goes undiagnosed and untreated.

In the United States, depression is estimated to cause two hundred million lost workdays each year. The Centers for Disease Control and Prevention (CDC) says this costs employers $17 billion to $44 billion.[4]

Depression is common, but it is also serious. It has been linked to other illnesses, including heart disease. Researchers have found that people who are depressed are more than twice as likely than others to develop high blood pressure, which is a major cause of heart disease. Even medium levels of anxiety and depression have been associated with a 60 percent greater likelihood of developing high blood pressure. A study out of Baltimore, Maryland, found that depressed people are four times more likely to have a heart attack than those with a more positive state of mind.[5] In addition, people who are depressed are more likely to smoke, which is another cause of heart disease and other serious health problems.

The greatest threat is the risk of suicide. Many people who are seriously depressed admit to having suicidal thoughts at some point, and all too many act on those thoughts.

Another way to look at the seriousness of depression is to consider how many people are being treated for the illness. The federal government has estimated that one in every ten Americans takes an antidepressant. The National Center for Health Statistics (NCHS) estimated that the rate of antidepressant use among young people increased by about 400 percent over two decades.[6]

## What Is Depression?

Winston Churchill, the famous British Prime Minister during World War II, called his depression his "black dog." It followed him throughout his life. So what is this thing called depression? The answer to that question is complicated. Some say depression is a physical illness; some say it is a psychological condition. Many say it depends. Sometimes it's mostly physical. Sometimes it's mostly psychological. Sometimes it's both. There may be several different kinds of depression with a combination of characteristics of both physical and mental illnesses or disorders.

For the purposes of this book, depression is defined as an illness or disorder that includes physical, emotional, and behavioral symptoms, such as changes in eating and sleeping patterns, overwhelmingly negative thoughts or feelings of hopelessness, and inability or limited ability to participate in activities that normally bring pleasure. When some combination of these symptoms lasts for an extended period of time—at least two weeks and often much longer—and it results in significant personal distress and interferes with normal functioning, depressive disorder is a likely diagnosis.

A depressive disorder is a group of symptoms that indicates a person has a sad mood that is beyond a normal period of feeling blue or feeling grief. Sometimes it is called major depressive disorder (MDD), unipolar disorder (as opposed to bipolar disorder, which is described in Chapter 6), clinical depression, or affective disorder (affective means having to do with emotions).

The word mood describes feelings that affect our attitude toward ourselves, our behavior toward others, and our ability to get work done, relax, or have fun. When good things happen to us, we usually react by being in a good mood. When we experience a lot of problems, disappointments, or losses, it is normal to be in a bad mood. Our mood tends to be a reaction to what happens to us.

Depression is what happens when an individual's mood response is not "normal." It is more than feeling sadness or even grief. Sadness that comes from loss is a normal part of everyone's life. Everyone has felt down about something; everyone has experienced the hurt of having best friends move away or decide they don't like us anymore. First relationships with a boyfriend or girlfriend usually end. Perhaps a beloved pet or a family member dies. Sadness is a natural human response to such situations, but that sadness is normally felt for a limited period of time, and gradually people are able to return to a good mood.

This book is about what happens when those feelings of a bad mood reach the level of disorder or illness, when the depressive state cannot be attributed to a particular loss, when it is out of proportion to a loss, or when the state goes on and on. This book is also about what can be done about depression. The good news is that many individuals are being successfully treated for depressive disorder. They can control the depression. They can go to school and work; they get on with their lives. And that, ultimately, is the purpose of this book—to help readers understand depression, recognize it in themselves or others, and learn how and where to find help.

## A Melancholy Journey

Depression and other mood disorders are not new. Countless individuals throughout history have struggled to lead successful lives while dealing with depression. Among them have been ordinary men and women, as well as great leaders and thinkers, including American President Abraham Lincoln. Lincoln was haunted by dreams and thoughts of death and dying.

Our understanding of depression and related illnesses has changed and developed over time. The ancient Greek storyteller Homer explained mental disorder as what happened when the gods took away a person's ability to think clearly. The philosopher Hippocrates described an illness called melancholy that included physical and emotional problems caused, in part, by having too much of what was called black bile, which in Greek was *melas* for dark and *kholé* for bile. The Greek philosophers Socrates, Plato, and Aristotle thought that mental disorder had more to do with philosophy,

## Famous People Who Have Fought Depression

Depression does not discriminate. Even the rich and famous may suffer from the disease. Here are a few celebrities and historical figures who have dealt with depression at some point in their lives.

**Entertainers**

- Jon Hamm
- Winona Ryder
- Owen Wilson
- Roseanne Barr
- J. K. Rowling
- Marlon Brando
- Delta Burke
- Drew Carey
- Jim Carrey
- Rosie O'Donnell
- Judy Collins
- Sheryl Crow
- Patty Duke
- Carrie Fisher
- Harrison Ford
- Linda Hamilton
- Janet Jackson
- Billy Joel
- Catherine Zeta Jones
- Ashley Judd
- Heath Ledger
- Demi Lovato
- David Arquette
- Gwyneth Paltrow

**Jim Carrey**       **Janet Jackson**       **J. K. Rowling**

**Historial Figures**

Michelangelo
Isaac Newton
Ludwig van Beethoven
Abraham Lincoln
Winston Churchill
Calvin Coolidge

Princess Diana
Charles Dickinson
Ernest Hemingway
Leo Tolstoy
Vincent Van Gogh
Buzz Aldrin

Abraham Lincoln     Buzz Aldrin     Amanda Beard

**Athletes**

Terry Bradshaw (football player)
Earl Campbell (football player)
John Daly (golfer)
Andre Waters (football player)
Daryl Strawberry (Baseball player)
Ricky Williams (football player)
Amanda Beard (Olympic swimmer)
Greg Louganis (Olympic medal-winning diver)

Ricky Williams

or thinking about thinking, than medicine. They suggested that keeping a distance from life's emotions was the best way to deal with what we call depression.

In the Middle Ages in Europe, many aspects of life, including the treatment of illness, were closely connected to the teachings of the Church. Mental disorder was often seen as the work of evil beings. Being depressed was considered sinful. During the time known as the Renaissance, as writers and thinkers rediscovered ancient Greek ideas, there was a renewed interest in the Greek idea of melancholy. Numerous mental and physical illnesses were grouped together under the label melancholy. Even though knowledge of how the body and brain work was limited, doctors of that time understood that episodes of melancholy could recur and worsen over time. They knew that melancholy causes premature aging, that some forms of melancholy emerge in old age, and that melancholy leads to heart problems.

William Shakespeare, an English Renaissance author of plays and poems, wrote about some depressed characters. Hamlet, Prince of Denmark, is one of the best known. At the beginning of the play *Hamlet*, the prince's inky black cloak gave the sixteenth-century audience a clue to his mood. The people of London knew that the character was depressed, although they did not use the term depression in those days. For some during the Renaissance, being depressed was fashionable—it conveyed depth, soulfulness, and intellect.

In the 1700s, doctors in England experimented with using small amounts of electricity to shock the brains of depressed patients. The stories of Benjamin Franklin's experiments with lightning in colonial America are well known, but less well known is that he was shocked into unconsciousness (and experienced brief memory loss) during one of his electricity experiments. As a result, he is said to have recommended electric shock for the treatment of mental illness.[7] Other physicians and thinkers of the eighteenth century understood that exercise could help relieve depression, which has been shown to help many who have the condition. Samuel Johnson, an English poet of the 1700s, believed that the active rural life could keep depression at bay compared to a more sedentary city life.

Another one of America's founding fathers, Benjamin Rush—a doctor who was also a signer of the Declaration of Independence—understood that there was a connection between the body and the mind. He argued that the mentally ill should be treated with respect, which was not often the case in those days. Rush received money from the state of Pennsylvania to improve care for mental patients. He believed in talking with patients to understand their illnesses.

**Depression is a relatively common mood disorder. But what is the difference between depression and simply feeling sad or melancholy, particularly during the difficult teenage years?**

His book *Medical Inquiries and Observations Upon the Diseases of the Mind*, published in 1812, earned him the title Father of American Psychiatry.

In 1895, German psychiatrist Emil Kraeplin began to categorize types of depression in terms of severity. He saw manic depression as different from schizophrenia, for example. He believed the cause was physical and might be treated medically.

In the early 1900s, the German psychiatrist Sigmund Freud began developing his theory of mental disorder. He believed that mental disorder arises from repression, or trying to hide or push away unwelcome or painful thoughts. Freud believed that repression is governed by the unconscious mind—thoughts that most people are not even aware of. According to Freud, too much repression leads to mental illness. Recovery, Freud believed, comes from examining the experiences of childhood through a process he developed and called psychoanalysis. In psychoanalysis, a patient lies on a couch and talks to the doctor about feelings and memories.

Freud's views influenced the way mental illness was treated for many years. Eventually, however, a growing number of people thought that the therapy took too long, cost too much, and produced little success, so new approaches came along.

In the meantime, a treatment more sophisticated than the experiments of the 1700s called electroshock therapy became a fairly common treatment for depression and other psychological disorders. As delivered in the mid-1900s, this treatment could be rough on the patient. Electroshock therapy is still used today with severely depressed patients and with those who are suicidal.

## The Power of the Pill

In time, scientists developed antidepressant medications that were less costly than some other options and easy for a patient to take. Medication is the most common way to treat depression today.

*Into the Bleak*

Scores of historical figures and fictional characters have suffered from depression. Shakespeare's character Hamlet is one example. Today, Hamlet would be diagnosed with clinical depression.

For example, in the 1940s a drug called Thorazine (chlorpromazine) was developed to treat schizophrenia, a devastating mental illness in which the patient is often out of touch with reality. The success of this drug in treating a psychiatric disorder brought hope that medicines could help treat illnesses of the mind.

In time, more successes were recorded. Researchers found links between body chemistry and mood. In the 1950s, research by Swiss scientists led to the discovery of imipramine (marketed as Tofranil), a drug with antidepressant, or depression-reducing, effects.

In the late 1980s and early 90s, new effective antidepressants came on the market, including Prozac (fluoxetine), Zoloft (sertraline), and Paxil (paroxetine). These medications have been incredibly popular with annual sales topping $1 billion. There has been backlash against such medicines, however. For many, it seemed that Prozac was being overprescribed. Some criticized that the pill was being given as a quick fix for more complex and severe forms of depression.

Some studies showed that patients might be experiencing a positive effect from antidepressants due to positive thinking. In 1997, psychologist Irving Kirsch gave placebos to patients with depression. Placebos are fake medications. Many of the patients felt their moods improve simply because they believed they were taking helpful medication.[8] A 2010 follow-up study confirmed that placebos might help those with mild and moderate depression but not those with more severe depression.

New and different forms of antidepressant medications continue to be introduced. In 2002, the US Food and Drug Administration (FDA) approved aripiprazole (brand name Abilify). This is an antipsychotic medication, but doctors have found that it can boost the effectiveness of antidepressants. In 2008, the FDA approved desvenlafaxine (Pristiq). In 2013, the FDA greenlighted vortioxetine (brand name Brintellix). These are a few of the more recent treatments for depression.[9]

To create an organized way of explaining mental disorders, an organization of psychiatrists called the American Psychiatric Association created a document called the *Diagnostic and Statistical Manual of Mental Disorders*. This manual, known as the *DSM*, was first published in 1952. It described 106 categories of mental disorders and was 130 pages long. As additional studies were done and new ways of thinking about mental illness developed, the *DSM* was revised. New editions were published: *DSM-II, DSM-III, DSM-III-R, DSM-IV, DSM-IV-TR*, and most recently, *DSM-5*, which was published in 2013.[10] In that edition, there are approximately three hundred disorders covered in more than eight hundred pages.

# Recognizing the Signs

Depression is an illness that affects people emotionally, physically, and mentally. Those with the sickness, however, experience it in different ways. Some may lash out with anger. Some may withdraw. Some, such as Kevin Breel, may keep it hidden inside. It can be difficult to pin down.

Sometimes an episode of depression is so dark and dramatic that no one can miss it. In other cases, it might seem to creep along just enough to keep a person feeling down most of the time but not unable to function. As one sufferer said, it can be "like having a constant low-grade fever."[1] People with depression describe a world drained of color, where life seems stale and empty. Problems are overwhelming, and there doesn't seem to be any light at the end of the tunnel.[2]

Just as the symptoms of various illnesses can be mistaken for the flu or a cold, the symptoms of depression have at times been confused with those of attention deficit disorder, drug and alcohol abuse, and other such complex problems. Our understanding of depression and these other disorders continues to develop. All these factors and others contribute to a many-layered description of depression.

Depression is generally considered a syndrome; that is, it includes a variety of symptoms. Not every individual diagnosed with depression experiences all the symptoms, but each has some of them. Sometimes the symptoms of depression are grouped by how they affect us: cognitive (how we think), behavioral (how we act), physical (how our body functions), and emotional (how we feel). Cognitive symptoms may include mental confusion, difficulty concentrating, extremely negative thoughts such as being highly self-critical, and perhaps thoughts of death. Depressed people may think about things that did not concern them before they were depressed. Many find themselves having the same disturbing thoughts again and again; these types of thoughts are known as obsessions.

Behavioral symptoms may include things that people do, such as crying a lot, as well as things avoided. For instance, a depressed person may not want to participate in activities that would normally be enjoyable.

Physical problems may include extreme tiredness and sleep problems, including both wanting to sleep all the time or not being able to sleep much at all, and weight changes related to eating a great deal less or a great deal more than normal. Physical problems can also include pain not explained by injury.

The emotional symptoms of depression are perhaps the most familiar: feelings of extreme sadness, hopelessness, irritability, panic, guilt, and anger. These feelings do not readily go away. Sometimes, however, the feeling most associated with severe depression is a huge emptiness, a lack of strong feelings about anything, a numbness, or a feeling of nothingness.

As one woman said, "When I became depressed, I had no emotions at all. I always delighted at spring before. But when I was depressed, I could look at the blooms and know it was beautiful, but I had no enjoyment of it." After she started taking medication and her depression began to lift, she said, "I just started feeling again."[3]

Many people reading about these symptoms might recognize feelings that they've had. Everybody experiences some of these symptoms at some time. Bad things happen, and we react to them. The factors that separate depressive illness from the normal ups and downs of life are the intensity of the symptoms, how deeply we experience them, how much they interfere with life, and how long they last.

So how does a person know if what he or she is experiencing is truly depressive disorder? A person who suspects a broken bone can get an X-ray to know for sure and decide what to do about it. For depression, as with most psychiatric disorders, there is, unfortunately, no quick and easy X-ray or lab test to show for sure what is wrong. Many of the symptoms overlap with the symptoms of other illnesses or conditions, and a diagnosis depends on what the patient can report and what a health care professional, and perhaps friends and family of the patient, can observe.

## Knowing for Sure

If a person thinks that he or she has the signs of depression, the next step is to see a health care professional to officially diagnose or label the problem. There are several different kinds of professionals to choose from, but the diagnostic process generally includes seeing someone who is a medical doctor, or MD. General practitioners, family physicians, and psychiatrists are all MDs. That means that, among other things, they can prescribe medicine, if needed.

A medical doctor can rule out illnesses that might look like depression, such as multiple sclerosis, over- or underactive thyroid, or mononucleosis. There may be other underlying causes of depression—heart problems, Parkinson's disease, or alcoholism. A family doctor who already knows a patient can be a good place to

*Recognizing the Signs*

start to help diagnose and treat the illness. If more intensive care is needed, the family doctor can then recommend a specialist.

A psychiatrist is a medical doctor who specializes in the treatment of illnesses involving emotion, behavior, and mental functioning. Persons studying to become psychiatrists go to medical school first and then continue with their education to learn about the diagnosis and treatment of psychiatric illnesses.

## Health Care Specialists

Note that MD is short for doctor of medicine, an academic degree.

| Specialist | MD? | Description |
| --- | --- | --- |
| General practitioner (GP) or family physician | Yes | A doctor who is generally considered a primary care physician; the person patients see for general illness and preventive care |
| Psychiatrist | Yes | A doctor who specializes in diagnosis and treatment of mental and emotional illness |
| Psychologist | Maybe | Mental health care provider trained in psychology; may have a doctoral degree (PhD) but most likely is not a trained medical doctor (MD) |
| Counselor | No | A National Certified Counselor (NCC) has a graduate degree in counseling and experience in settings such as marriage and family or addiction treatment |

Because there is no simple laboratory test to tell if someone has depression, the psychiatrist has to gather a lot of other information to help make a diagnosis. He or she asks about the patient's family medical history. Mood problems in relatives can help make the diagnosis of a mood disorder more likely. Questions and answers about the patient's mood, appetite, daily activity levels, and sleep habits help with the diagnosis. The psychiatrist also asks about the patient's relationships and about how the individual is getting along with others.

Psychologists usually have an advanced degree called a PhD, which gives them the title of doctor, but usually they are not MDs, or medical doctors. In some states, individuals need only a bachelor's degree or master's degree in psychology to be called a psychologist. Because psychologists are not medical doctors, they cannot prescribe medicine, order lab tests, or perform physical exams. A psychologist focuses on what is going on in the mind of the patient rather than on an illness.

## Categories of Depression

In cases of mental and emotional disorders, just as in physical illness, an accurate diagnosis helps determine the best treatment. That's where the *DSM*, or the *Diagnostic and Statistical Manual of Mental Disorders* described in Chapter 1, comes in.

The *DSM* places disorders into categories and groups of categories. One of the categories is mood disorders. Depressive disorders are found in this category. Other mood disorders include bipolar disorders, mood disorders due to a medical condition, and mood disorders due to substance abuse. These other types of mood disorders will be discussed in Chapter 6.

There are several kinds of depressive disorders listed in the *DSM*. These include major depression, dysthymia (a more chronic or ongoing form of depression that is generally not as severe at all times as major depression but usually lasts longer), and depressive disorder NOS (not otherwise specified).

*Recognizing the Signs*

The inability to concentrate on tasks such as homework can be indicative of depression. However, since many people find homework less than captivating, other symptoms need to be present.

Some doctors think that some people experience depression that is a blend of these categories. Major depression is what we generally mean when we talk about serious depression or depression as an illness or disorder. According to 2012 statistics from Substance Abuse and Mental Health Services, 8.4 percent of women and 5.2 percent of men had an episode of major depression in the past year.[4]

Not every individual with depression has all these symptoms, but to be diagnosed with major depressive disorder (MDD) according to the *DSM*, an individual must have at least five symptoms most of the time for a period of two weeks or longer. To be diagnosed with dysthymia, fewer symptoms may be present, and they may not be

*Are You Depressed?*

## Questions Asked to Diagnose Depression

Here are a few questions that a health care provider may ask to establish if a patient has depression.

- Has depression been diagnosed and treated in this individual before?
- Have relatives been treated for depression?
- What physical and emotional symptoms have been experienced?
- How long has the individual been feeling this way?
- How severe are the symptoms? How much do they interfere with daily life?
- Are thoughts about death or suicide present?

present as much of the time, but they must have been felt for two years or more.

Although we usually think of the feelings of sadness as the most obvious signs of depression, sometimes another symptom sends a person to the doctor only to find depression at the root of the problem. According to data collected by the World Health Organization (WHO), of nearly twenty-six thousand people who had seen a doctor, 69 percent of those diagnosed with depression reported only physical, not emotional, problems. In other words, physical discomfort prompted them to seek medical help. Physical symptoms of depression can be changes in weight, sleep, or appetite. Fatigue, headaches, backaches, problems with digestion, or menstrual issues may also be indicators. In this WHO report, 11 percent did not report any psychological symptoms even when asked about them.[5] Perhaps they did not want to talk about emotional symptoms, or maybe physical symptoms bothered them most.

*Recognizing the Signs*

The first symptoms of **depression** can sometimes be physical and not emotional. Depression can manifest itself in headaches and problems with digestion.

## Signs of Depression

The American Psychiatric Association's *DSM-5* lists the following symptoms that may indicate a major depressive episode if they are present during a two-week period. Note that these symptoms may be observed by the individual or an observation made by others.

- Depressed mood most of the day nearly every day. For example, there may be feelings of emptiness or sadness.
- A noticeable diminished interest or pleasure in all, or almost all, activities most of the day nearly every day.
- Significant weight loss when not dieting or weight gain. (This would be a change of at least 5 percent in body weight in a month.)
- A decrease or increase in appetite nearly every day.
- Insominia (difficulty sleeping) or hypersomnia (excessive sleepiness).
- Fatigue or loss of energy nearly every day.
- Feeling worthless or overly or inappropriately guilty nearly every day.
- Psychomotor agitation (a restlessness) or retardation (a lethargy) almost every day.
- Difficulty concentrating.
- Thoughts of death or suicide that keep coming back.[6]

## Depression Does Not Discriminate

Depression affects people of both genders, as well as people from many different social and cultural backgrounds. It occurs in the young, the old, and every age group in between.

**Children and Adolescents.** Many people are surprised to learn that even young children can suffer from depression. One doctor at New York University's Child Study Center estimated that one in forty babies might get depression.[7] A 2009 investigation of more than three hundred preschoolers found that some children as young as three years old had symptoms of depression.[8] The National Association of School Psychologists (NASP) estimates that 1 percent of preschool children and 2 percent of prepuberty age children may suffer from a major depressive disorder. Just more than one in ten adolescents have a depressive disorder by age eighteen, according to the National Comorbidity Survey—Adolescent Supplement.[9] Girls are more likely to experience this illness than boys. Suicide is the third leading cause of death among youth ages fifteen to twenty-four.[10]

Like everyone else, most children react with sadness when something goes wrong at home or school. When children have the blues, their sad feelings usually begin to lessen within a few days. If their sadness increases, lasts for more than two weeks, or if other symptoms of depression develop, the situation may call for outside help. Depression in children should not be ignored because a child who experiences serious depression is at greater risk for having additional episodes later in life and for developing other problems, such as uncontrollable fears, or phobias.

Another problem is that young children may not have the vocabulary to describe their changes in mood, and they may have trouble getting help. A concerned adult noticing dramatic changes in behavior can sometimes be the key to the diagnosis of depression in children.

Also, symptoms may be hard to recognize. In young children, depression may display itself as a lack of playfulness, phobias, aggressive behavior, or clinginess. NASP says that as children grow older, they may express morbid thoughts, worry about school, have trouble sleeping, or blame themselves for disappointing their parents and teachers.

Because even under the best of circumstances the teenage years can be difficult, it can be all too easy to mistake the symptoms of depression for ordinary teenage problems. Like young children, adolescents may find it difficult to put their feelings into words, which further complicates the situation. Behavioral changes may be the most prominent symptoms, but again, virtually all teenagers try out different behaviors from time to time. Some behaviors, though, such as substance abuse, extreme risk taking, or violence toward themselves or others, are always causes for concern.

**Men and women.** Both men and women can experience depression, but women experience twice the rate of depression as men regardless of race or ethnic background, according to the National Alliance on Mental Illness. There may be several reasons. Some experts believe women experience depression more often because of physical factors, such as changes in chemicals in the body called hormones. Others feel that the different ways men and women are taught to deal with emotions in our culture explain differences in depression in men and women. Some see other factors, such as poverty or abuse, as being important. Depression may be the result of such traumatic life events.

One kind of depression unique to women is what is often called the baby blues, or postpartum depression. Within a couple of days after having a baby, some women experience crying spells and a feeling of unexplained sadness. That feeling seems directly connected to the hormonal changes in a woman's body following pregnancy and childbirth. Thankfully, in most cases the feeling passes without harm. But in a small percentage of cases, the feeling may be a symptom of a more dangerous form of the illness called postpartum psychosis. That form can cause serious problems for the mother and baby. In some cases it has been linked to the mother

*Recognizing the Signs*

Clinging to a parent can be a symptom of depression in children. Other symptoms are prolonged sadness, morbid thoughts, and avoidance of playtime.

*Are You Depressed?*

harming her child. About 2 to 10 percent of women experience Premenstrual Dysphoric Disorder, a severe form of premenstrual syndrome (PMS) that can severely impair behavior and create drastic mood changes. [11]

**The elderly.** Some people seem to expect older persons to be depressed since our society typically places less value on this time of life. In fact, a great many older Americans do suffer from depression. Some estimate that major depression in older people ranges from less than 1 percent to about 5 percent of this population. Among those who require home health care, about 13.5 percent may be depressed, and about 11.5 percent of older hospital patients may have depression. Doctors stress, however, that depression does not have to be a normal part of aging. [12]

## The Root of the Blues

Why do people get depressed? The illness can be brought on by a number of different factors. A loss in a person's life can bring it on suddenly, or the illness can slowly build over time. Brain chemistry, genes, and other medical conditions can play a role. Even daylight or lack of it can be at the root of feeling extremely down. Most often, depression seems to worsen over time, and without treatment it can last for months or sometimes much longer.

Research has shown that once someone experiences a major depressive episode, he or she is at an increased risk of experiencing depression again. In other words, depression tends to recur. At least half of those who recover from an episode of depression have one or more additional episodes in their lifetime. About eight out of ten of those with a history of two episodes have yet another recurrence.[1] In fact, when many people seek help for depression, doctors find that the patient has experienced this problem in the past.

Theories about the origins of depression continue to change, and those involved in the research and treatment of depression continue to debate them. Most experts believe that no single cause explains all cases of depression. Instead depression results from a combination of physical and psychological factors, and the particular combination of those factors varies from person to person.

Often a serious loss or unpleasant experience seems to trigger an episode of depression, but the actual cause is more complex. Something in that individual's personality, heredity, or biology sets the stage for depression. One or more of those factors may come into play for any particular case of depression.

Sometimes the onset of depression is compared to the way we catch a cold. We are told not to go outside in a cold rain or we might catch a cold, although we know that viruses cause colds and not weather. But going out in a cold rain and getting chilled just might trigger a virus to make us sick. In a similar way, a devastating loss might be a trigger that brings on a case of major depression.

## A Matter of Brain Communication

Scientists know that different parts of the brain play different roles in the way we think, feel, and behave. Something that goes wrong in one part of the brain can change the particular kind of thinking, emotion, or behavior that is linked to that part of the brain. For the last four decades of the twentieth century, researchers studied brain chemistry for clues about what was happening in the brain of a depressed person. This research led to the development of a theory linking depression to certain chemicals in the brain called neurotransmitters. Neurotransmitters are messenger molecules; they are important in the process of communication between cells in the brain. For example, neurotransmitters tell the heart to beat, the lungs to breathe, and the stomach to digest.

The brain and the rest of the nervous system have been compared to a large collection of electric or telephone wires or to a complicated network of computers. In the brain, electrical signals

*The Root of the Blues*

The loss of a loved one can trigger depression, but such experiences are rarely the root of the problem.

travel along nerve fibers until they reach the end of that cell. A chemical messenger carries the signal across the space at the end of each nerve to the next one. This messenger is the neurotransmitter. Neurotransmitters move across the space between nerve cells and match up with the surface of the next cell. Then the electrical signal continues down the next nerve cell. And on and on. Once the neurotransmitter's work is done, it either gets absorbed into a nerve cell or is broken down by other chemicals that clean up the space between the cells.

Researchers have concluded that mood changes may be the result of changes in the amounts of neurotransmitters in the brain. If there isn't enough of the right kind of neurotransmitters, messages can't pass between nerve cells, and communication in the brain slows down. One result of this lack of communication in the brain might be an episode of major depression.

## Three Important Brain Chemicals

There are many different kinds of neurotransmitters, but the ones that seem to be most closely linked to depression are norepinephrine, serotonin, and dopamine. Studies from the 1960s and 1970s noted that certain drugs that reduced serotonin and norepinephrine levels in the brain could result in depression in some individuals. On the other hand, medications that increase levels of these neurotransmitters seem to decrease depression in some people.

The theory that the kinds and amounts of neurotransmitters in the brain are directly related to depression is called the monoamine hypothesis of depression. (Neurotransmitters are in a chemical group called monoamines.) It is one of the most heavily studied theories of depression. By itself, however, the monoamine hypothesis does not answer all questions about the cause of depression. Some new antidepressant medications have little effect on the level of neurotransmitters, yet they relieve depression. And some other drugs, which are known to impact neurotransmitters, have not been successful in the treatment of depression. Even if the

*The Root of the Blues*

theory is correct, it is a mystery why the level of neurotransmitters in the brain can rise quite quickly, but the beneficial response to drugs generally takes at least two weeks to become evident.

## Hormones and Other Causes

There are other theories about how things happening in the body can affect mood and perhaps cause depression. Studies have looked at the connection between hormones in the body and depression. The neurotransmitters norepinephrine, serotonin, and dopamine play a part in the release of hormones. Hormones, in turn, affect the activity of neurotransmitters. Deficiencies in certain hormones have

**Studies show that the switch that controls synapses in the brain can be overproduced in people who suffer from depression. This affects cell-to-cell communication and results in depressive behavior.**

been associated with dramatic mood changes. Doctors have often noticed that people who suffer from diseases of the thyroid and adrenal glands, which produce hormones, have many symptoms similar to those of depression. Stress can cause the release of hormones that may act in some way to cause depression.

Another line of research looks at parts of the brain that are involved in higher order thinking and emotional processing: the prefrontal and limbic regions. These regions are highly interconnected by networks of nerve cells. Studies have looked at how malfunctions in these connections can result in the symptoms of major depression.

Scientists continue to study every aspect of the brain, as well as interactions between the brain and other systems in the body, to find answers. Results have yielded some interesting information, but there are still many questions to answer.

## It's in the Genes

Some families have more members with depressive disorder than others. This observation has led researchers to look for genetic causes for depression.

Genetics is the study of inherited characteristics. An Austrian monk named Gregor Mendel performed some famous experiments in the 1860s that showed some traits, such as color in garden peas, seem to be determined by a single pair of genes. This is called a simple inheritance pattern. Some human traits, such as blood type, follow simple inheritance patterns.

Most human traits, however, seem to be determined by a combination of several or many genes. Depression is likely to fall into this category because while there does seem to be some connection between genetics and depression, family history is not an automatic predictor. In other words, just because a parent has depression doesn't necessarily mean the children will, as well. Instead, depression and other mood disorders fall into the category of inherited traits for which only rough estimates can be made about the chances of inheriting the disorder.

For example, individuals who have what's called a first-degree relative, such as a parent or brother or sister, with major depression are 1.5 to 3 times more likely as the general population to also have major depression. The Stanford School of Medicine in Palo Alto, California, says that in most cases of depression, about 50 percent of the cause is genetic and around 50 percent is unrelated to genes, such as psychological or physical factors.[2]

People with a history of mood disorders in their families should not hesitate to seek help if they see symptoms of depression or other mood disorders in themselves.

## Psychology May Play a Role

There is also evidence that depression can develop from psychological causes. Psychological trauma experienced in childhood can have an effect on a child that results in depression then or later in life. Research has found that early adversity may disrupt the development of social and personal coping skills. For example, if a child loses a parent at a young age, this traumatic experience can lead to depression.

## The Depression Gene

In 2011, British scientists discovered a gene that appears frequently in multiple family members who have depression. Chromosome 3p25-26 was found in more than eight hundred families with repeating episodes of depression. These researchers say that as much as 40 percent of depression can be traced to a genetic connection.[3]

## Are You Depressed?

It is believed that 50 percent of depression is genetic. If you have a first-degree relative with depression, such as a parent or sibling, you are more likely to have depression.

***Reduced personal resources.*** When certain personal resources suffer due to a traumatic incident or difficulties, the risk of depression can rise. Two personal resources are mastery and self-esteem. Mastery refers to whether people believe that they have control over the situations in which they find themselves. The degree to which a person feels in control has a big impact on how he or she copes with a situation. Mastery helps individuals handle stressful situations or avoid them in the first place. People who believe that problems are caused by outside forces beyond their control are likely to experience more stress. As a result, they may not even try to solve problems that come up in their lives. "Why bother?" they may think. Children who grow up in highly stressful home environments tend to perform poorly in school compared to other children. There seems to be a link between a difficult childhood and an inability to improve one's life.[4]

Self-esteem is a concept familiar to most people. It includes how individuals look at themselves, as well as how individuals compare themselves to others. Certain circumstances in children's lives can directly reduce self-esteem and predict later mental health outcomes. Researchers have found that children who are abused physically, mentally, or sexually are more likely to have poor self-esteem and mental health problems as they grow up.[5]

Situations of adversity that go on throughout childhood and adolescence may be interpreted as evidence that individuals cannot change the difficult situations of their lives. Strong evidence links these feelings of helplessness with the symptoms of depression. Support from parents and other family members can help reduce the negative impact of childhood adversity. But if the family is the source of the adversity or if the adversity is the loss of family (through death or divorce, for example), then a child may face insurmountable obstacles. Stopping the downward path that begins with a childhood of adversity can help pave the way to a happier life.

***Distorted thinking.*** Sometimes depression develops in the absence of childhood trauma. In these cases, distorted or mistaken patterns of thinking may have developed through ordinary living.

When there is a loss or traumatic event, these distorted thoughts lead to problems. If someone loses something important to them, such as a job or a relationship, and blames himself or herself unfairly for what happened, depression may be the result. The fact that others may place no blame on the person for the setbacks often makes no difference.

The age at which the combination of loss and distorted thoughts strikes can have a big impact. If a great loss combined with unfair self-blame occurs at an early age before a child has developed good coping behaviors, the stage may be set for trouble. Early loss of a parent and childhood health problems may predict later episodes of depression. Romantic break-ups are sometimes associated with the onset of first episodes of depression in adolescents—a result, perhaps, of a fragile self-image at this time in life that makes negative thoughts directed inward more common.

Studies have consistently shown that people who experience significant negative life events are more likely to suffer from depression.[6] But it is not necessarily the reaction to negative life events that is the problem but rather the reaction to the reaction. In other words, grief following the loss is not the problem, but how a person copes with the grief is. If coping involves distorted thinking, depression may develop.

***Avoidance.*** Depression often develops when, after a loss of some type, negative feelings are turned inward against the person who has suffered the loss. That can lead to a behavior called avoidance, and avoidance can lead to depression.

Avoidance is when a person avoids, stays away from, or denies something that causes distress. For example, if you play with matches and burn yourself, you will hopefully learn that playing with matches is harmful, and you will avoid that behavior due to its consequences.

**Children raised in abusive homes are more apt to suffer from depression later in life. The low self-esteem that results from abuse is associated with adult mental disorders.**

The behavior that is maintained then is not playing with matches. This is functional avoidance. It is good for you; it helps you survive.

At other times, avoidance is dysfunctional, and it is not good for you. This can lead to mental disorders, such as anxiety disorders and depression. For example, some people experience phobias, which are extreme fears of things not generally considered harmful. People with phobias often exhibit avoidance behavior that can have negative consequences. An example is a fear of cars so extreme that a person cannot stand to get in one to go anywhere. Avoidance becomes dysfunctional when its long-term consequences are negative or harmful. Depression may be brought on by dysfunctional avoidance behaviors, including avoiding activities that would help combat the depression.

*Negative thoughts.* A related idea to distorted thinking is a concept called negative thinking. This is a tendency to attribute problems unfairly to weaknesses in oneself that are considered permanent and unchangeable. In other words, the individual decides that he or she is a failure or a loser and that nothing can be done about it. This type of thinking can lead to an inability to cope, hopelessness, and depression.

Some individuals find that one particular negative thought haunts them day and night when they are having a depressive episode. This same thought does not bother them at other times. It is amazing to see how these mountains shrink to their true molehill size as the depression lifts.[7] People may find it hard to believe how upset they were by that thought once they feel better. Sometimes people can tell that an episode of depression is about to begin when a particular thought or set of thoughts starts bugging them.

## A Troubled Sleep Can Lead to a Troubled Mind

There is a complicated connection between depression and sleep disorders. Some people become depressed first and then develop sleeping problems. In other cases, difficulty sleeping leads to depression. Trying to figure out which came first can help determine which symptoms to treat first.

The Centers for Disease Control and Prevention reported in 2014 that people who don't get enough sleep are more likely to suffer from depression.[8] A poll from the National Sleep Foundation found that among children aged eleven to seventeen who reported being unhappy, 73 percent said they were not sleeping enough at night.[9]

## A Seasonal Sadness

In recent decades, some experts on depression have noticed that certain people are more likely to be depressed at certain times of the

**Many people with depression have trouble sleeping. Sometimes lack of sleep triggers depression, but depression can also be the cause of an inability to sleep soundly.**

year. This is called seasonal affective disorder, or SAD. Remember, affective refers to emotions. The disorder is connected to changes in sunlight levels that come with the seasons.

Typically, SAD is diagnosed when an individual experiences a strong connection between a change in mood and a particular time of the year. The change has to happen two years in a row plus a third year previously. The most common form of the illness is depression in winter (when there is less sunlight) and normal mood in summer (when there is more sunlight). The reverse pattern is true for some people and is still considered to be SAD.

According to information updated in 2014 in *Psychology Today*, about ten million Americans experience SAD, and an additional 10

*Are You Depressed?*

If you find yourself feeling sad, tired, and hopeless during the winter months you might be afflicted with seasonal affective disorder. Light therapy has proven to be an effective treatment for SAD.

to 20 percent may have a mild form of SAD. More women than men have the condition. Up to 6 percent of those with SAD have it so severely that they have to be hospitalized. Sometimes children and adolescents can have SAD, but it mostly occurs in those older than twenty, and it is more common the further north a person lives.[10]

SAD comes with all the symptoms of depressive disorder but with some variations. For example, with SAD, both appetite and need for sleep usually increase, while persons with non-light-related depressive disorder might eat and sleep very little. However, these changes can go either way in both kinds of depression. At the same time, persons with SAD generally experience the same kinds of feelings of guilt, hopelessness, and ongoing lowering of mood that accompany depressive disorder.

## When Illness Causes Depression Symptoms

A number of illnesses can produce the symptoms of depression—probably because those diseases cause the same changes in the brain as depression does. Patients experience more than being sad from being ill; they are ill and have the symptoms of depression, as well.

Addison's disease is one such illness. In Addison's disease, something causes the adrenal glands to shrink. As a result, levels of the hormones that are secreted by these glands fall, which in turn can produce weakness, loss of appetite, weight loss, and other symptoms common to major depression.

Mood is also closely tied to the workings of the thyroid system. Hypothyroidism results from a decrease in the hormone produced by the thyroid gland. Persons with hypothyroidism often show many of the symptoms of major depression.

The glands discussed here, the adrenal and thyroid, are regulated by the pituitary gland, which in turn receives signals from a part of the brain called the hypothalamus. Because all these systems are interconnected, problems with the pituitary gland and hypothalamus can also lead to depression.

Other illnesses can also include a seriously depressed mood as part of their symptoms. Parkinson's disease and Huntington's disease have devastating effects on the brain, and patients with those diseases can sometimes have episodes of major depression in the course of their illness. Multiple sclerosis, a disease of the nervous system, can cause dramatic mood changes.

Infections have also been linked to depression. Tuberculosis (an infection of the lungs), hepatitis (an infection of the liver), and mononucleosis (a viral infection that causes extreme tiredness), are often accompanied by depression. Lead poisoning can cause the symptoms of depression, too.

If so many diseases share symptoms with major depression, how do we know when the diagnosis should be depressive disorder and not some other illness? First of all, major depression is more common than these other illnesses. If a person has the symptoms of depression, depression is the most likely cause. Also, if the problem is actually one of the other diseases, other symptoms generally provide the doctor with clues. Those clues can lead to tests that confirm the diagnosis of some other illness.

## Feeling Down From Medications

Some people develop depression as a result of taking certain medications. Some of the drugs that have been linked to depression include sleeping pills, diet pills, birth control pills, and medications for high blood pressure, arthritis, ulcers, and seizures.

Steroid medications can cause severe mood changes. Because they are valuable anti-inflammatory agents that act against inflammation or irritation in the body, steroids have many uses in medicine, including treatment for joint and lung diseases, as well as some kinds of cancer.[11] (The steroid medications referred to here should not be confused with anabolic steroids, commonly known as performance-enhancing drugs. Anabolic steroids are sometimes used by athletes to build muscle artificially and to improve athletic performance, a practice that is neither legal nor safe.) Patients who take steroid medications should be alert for the symptoms of developing depression.

Steroids can cause mood changes in either direction—that is, they can cause either depression or the wild upward mood swing called euphoria. In fact, steroids can cause moods to swing first one way and then the other. When first started on a steroid, a patient may experience a state of high energy and happiness. That may last for a few days until the good feelings gradually slip away and depression sets in.

# A Prescription for Depression

After a health care provider has diagnosed an individual with depression, the patient has many potential options for treatment depending on the severity and kind of depression he or she has. While some may find approaches with diet and exercise can be enough to get back on track, many need more intensive treatment involving medication, mental thereapy, or other possible therapies.

Different kinds of health care professionals provide different kinds of treatments. For some people, understanding and dealing with the thinking patterns involved in depression are the most important parts of getting better. These patients might choose to see a psychiatrist, psychologist, or therapist to focus on psychological treatment. We will look at those treatments more closely in Chapter 5.

For others, the answer lies in finding out if there is something wrong with the way their brain chemistry is working. Once a good physical exam has ruled out another kind of illness as the problem, a medical doctor can offer treatment for depression with medication. A family doctor or general practitioner may prescribe an antidepressant, which is medication specifically for depression. Or the doctor may recommend a psychiatrist who can make the decision about antidepressant medication. A psychiatrist is a medical doctor, or MD, who specializes in care related to behavioral and emotional illness.

The key is to understand that help is available. While finding the right doctor and right treatment takes time, many people can be successfully treated—often within three to four months. The National Alliance on Mental Illness says that between 80 and 90 percent of individuals diagnosed with major depression can be effectively treated and return to their usual daily activities and feelings.[1]

## Medications for Better Moods

Increased understanding of how the brain works has led to the development of medications to help it work better. Some of those medications help ease the symptoms of depression. In Chapter 3 we looked at how an imbalance in certain chemicals called neurotransmitters seems to be related to the symptoms of depression. The chemicals that help fix this imbalance and ease the symptoms of depression are called antidepressants.

There are a number of different groups of antidepressants and a variety of medications in each group. The various groups tend to act on the brain in different ways. A doctor prescribing an antidepressant tries to match the needs of the patient with the right kind of medication.

Finding the right medication for a particular individual is not always easy. Doctors have a wide range of antidepressants to choose from, and the first one selected may not work. Sometimes a medication can cause new symptoms, called side effects, that can make the patient feel worse. Some studies show that the response

*A Prescription for Depression*

Medication can reduce the symptoms associated with depression. There are many different types of depression medication, and only a doctor is qualified to choose the right one for you.

rate to the first recommended antidepressant is somewhere around 50 percent.[2] A response does not necessarily mean that the depression goes away; it means only that the patient experiences at least some improvement. Many antidepressant medication statistics refer to this standard—that there is some improvement—and do not mean that depression is "cured."

The table Antidepressant Medications shows some of the kinds of antidepressants available today. Each of these groups is examined more closely later in this chapter. Tricyclic antidepressants were among the first developed. They treat depression by boosting the level of several different neurotransmitters in the brain, including norepinephrine, serotonin, and dopamine. They block the reabsorption of neurotransmitters back into the neuron that released them. SSRIs are similar except that they focus on one neurotransmitter, serotonin. MAOIs destroy enzymes responsible for breaking down neurotransmitters; that's how they increase neurotransmitter levels. All of the antidepressants can be effective

## Know the Meds

There are so many types of medications that keeping the names straight can sometimes be confusing. There are two basic types of drugs: brand name and generic. The brand name of a drug is the name given to it by the company that first manufactures it. The name begins with an uppercase letter like other proper nouns. The generic name of a drug begins with a lowercase letter, and it is the name of the drug's chemical formulation. For example, the generic drug fluvoxamine has the brand name Luvox.

In the United States, a new drug can be sold only by the company that invented it as long as the patent lasts—usually between seven and twelve years. After that time, generic versions of the drug can be made and marketed by other pharmaceutical companies. Generic drugs have the same active ingredients as the original drug but are cheaper.

## Antidepressant Medications

Here are some of the biggest categories of drugs used to treat depression.

| Kind | Generic name (brand name) | Description |
|---|---|---|
| SSRIs | fluoxetine (Prozac) paroxetine (Paxil) sertraline (Zoloft) | Prevent the reuptake, or absorption, of the neurotransmitter serotonin |
| Tricyclics | amitriptyline (Elavil, Endep, Vanatrip) desipramine (Norpramin) | Block the reuptake, or absorption, of several neurotransmitters |
| MAOIs | moclamine (Manerix) Phenelzine (Nardil) | Block enzymes (chemicals) that break down neurotransmitters |
| Others | bupropion (Wellbutrin) nefazondone (Serzone) venlafaxine (Effexor) | Affect brain chemistry in different ways |

in decreasing the symptoms of depression, such as feelings of hopelessness and extreme sadness, poor sleep and appetite, difficulty concentrating, lack of energy and interest, and so on.

Many people wonder how long they will have to take an antidepressant. These medications generally work for as long as they are taken; while they're in an individual's system, they affect the chemicals in the brain in a way that decreases the symptoms. That means that if an individual stops taking the medication, the symptoms of depression are likely to return, especially if the drug has been used for only a short while. Whatever was causing the depression in the first place is still there. If medications are taken for a

## Are You Depressed?

long enough time, however, the chemical imbalance or whatever led to the depression may have passed before the drug is discontinued.

In cases of major depression, medication is typically taken for about six months before a doctor suggests reducing the dose. If the symptoms return, the patient can go back to the original dosage. If the patient continues to feel better, then perhaps that episode of depression has passed. For milder but longer lasting forms of depression, a doctor may wait a year before reducing the dose.

Many doctors feel that a patient should not stop taking an antidepressant too soon. Studies have shown that as many as 70 percent of patients on antidepressants become depressed again if they stop taking their medication within five weeks of having the depression lift.[3] Those who continue taking the antidepressant for at least five months after their symptoms decrease are much less likely to have the depression return.

When it *is* time to stop taking the antidepressant, doctors generally recommend a gradual reduction to avoid unpleasant side effects, such as restlessness and anxiety.

Sometimes people worry about becoming addicted to a drug that they take for a long time. Antidepressants are not addictive. They can, however, cause side effects—some of which are minor annoyances, but some of which can be quite serious depending on which neurotransmitters are affected and how they are acted upon. Some common side effects of antidepressants include sleepiness or insomnia (difficulty sleeping), dry mouth, constipation, and dizziness. Sometimes the side effects can be lessened by taking the medication before bed—unless the side effect is insomnia! As Dr. Francis Mark Mondimore, author of *Depression, the Mood Disease*, states, "Side effects do not mean you must stop taking the drug. Rather, it means you have a decision to make: Am I willing to put up with the side effects of this medication to get the antidepressant effect?"[4]

Sometimes a second drug is combined with the first, which reduces the amount needed of each and lessens side effects.

*A Prescription for Depression*

Some research indicates that about 66 percent of individuals with depression respond to a single antidepressant, and nearly 95 percent respond to a combination of antidepressants.[5] Remember, this is a response and not necessarily a complete recovery.

## Carefully Weighing the Pros and Cons

Use of antidepressants has increased dramatically in the last few decades as newer medications have been developed that have fewer side effects and as studies indicate the effectiveness of the medications. Some people find this increased use worrisome, especially because the prescribing of antidepressants for children and adolescents has also increased. Whether antidepressant medication for the young is a good thing is the subject of debate. On the one hand, few people argue with the idea of helping children with depression. On the other hand, little is known about the long-term effects of antidepressants on developing minds and bodies.

While there is also concern about the risks for pregnant women who take antidepressants, there are also concerns about serious risks for women with depression who go untreated during pregnancy. A pregnant woman who is depressed must work with her doctor to weigh all the risk factors and reach a decision about what is best for her and her baby.

Some people are skeptical of the effectiveness of these medications. They think that antidepressants are simply happy pills. Researchers counter that antidepressants won't make healthy people feel a false high as certain illegal drugs can. If you don't have a neurotransmitter problem causing you to feel depressed, it's unlikely that taking an antidepressant will affect the way you feel.

Some therapists doubt whether antidepressants are the best way to treat depression. According to the authors of *The Myth of Depression as Disease*, "Medications are one option, but outcomes may be shorter lived than those found with behavioral therapies, and there are significant adverse side effects associated with medications."[6] Still, many individuals report that they are able to live a full and happy life with the aid of antidepressants.

## Selective Serotonin Reuptake Inhibitors (SSRIs)

Drugs in the SSRI group are most commonly prescribed for depression today. In general, these medications are safer and cause fewer side effects than other options. One in particular, known by the brand name Prozac (generic name fluoxetine), is the most popular of the SSRIs. In 2010, more than 24.4 million prescriptions for fluoxetine were filled.[7] Some estimates indicate that more than 70 percent have seen improvement in their depression.[8] Other drugs in this group are Celexa (citalopram), Lexapro (escitalopram), Luvox (fluvoxamine), Zoloft (sertraline), and Paxil (paroxetine).

SSRI stands for selective serotonin reuptake inhibitor. SSRIs slow down the absorption of serotonin. After serotonin has done its work as a messenger in the brain, it is absorbed by brain cells to be used another time. This is called reuptake. When this process is slowed down, or inhibited, more serotonin is left to send messages. Therefore, a drug that selectively inhibits the reuptake of serotonin is a selective serotonin reuptake inhibitor.

These drugs act on only one neurotransmitter. SSRIs are also used to treat other disorders in addition to depression, including obsessive-compulsive disorder (OCD), eating disorders, social phobia, anxiety or panic disorders, and posttraumatic stress disorder. SSRIs may be the safest antidepressants for heart patients because the drugs do not interfere with blood pressure or heart functioning the way some other antidepressants can.

Fewer side effects are one of the main reasons for the popularity of SSRIs, but side effects do occur. Like most antidepressants, SSRIs may cause nausea, dizziness, dry mouth, and other problems. Because these drugs are relatively new, there is some concern about the possibility of long-term effects that won't show up until later, though none are known at this time. Also, because they are newer, SSRIs tend to be more expensive than the older antidepressants,

## A Prescription for Depression

SSRIs treat depression by slowing down the absorption of serotonin in the brain. SSRIs, such as Prozac, Soloft, and Lexapro, are prescribed for depression, eating disorders, PTSD, and anxiety.

which are more likely to be available in generic, or nonbrand-name, form.

## Tricyclics

Before the past fifty years or so, psychiatrists treating depressed patients usually had to rely on either psychoanalysis as developed by Sigmund Freud or on electroshock therapy, which was much more traumatic at that time than it is today. In the 1950s, Swiss scientists researching drugs to treat the psychological illness schizophrenia found that a medication called imipramine (sold under the brand name Tofranil) seemed to perk up depressed patients. It became the first of a group of antidepressants that are called tricyclics because they have a three-ring chemical structure. These drugs, plus the four-ring tetracyclics, are together called cyclic antidepressants.

Besides Tofranil, popular tricyclics include Pamelor (nortriptyline), Surmontil (trimipramine), Norpramin (desipramine), and Vivactil (protriptyline). Compared to newer antidepressants, they cause

## Ask About Antidepressant Medications

A patient who is considering taking an antidepressant should ask the following questions of their health care provider.

- Why is this the best drug for me?
- What side effects are likely to occur? What can be done about them?
- Is it okay to take this with any other medications I am taking?
- What time of day should I take the antidepressant, and should I take it with or without food?
- What should I do if I miss a dose?
- How long will I take this medication before I can expect to know if it's working? How will I know?

more side effects. Doctors tend not to prescribe these unless SSRIs do not work, according to the Mayo Clinic.[9]

Tricyclic antidepressants slow the process by which certain neurotransmitters are reabsorbed into brain cells after they do their messenger work. Tricyclics primarily block the reuptake of norepinephrine and serotonin, which results in an increase in the levels of these neurotransmitters in the brain and a decrease in the symptoms of depression. Patients usually report a gradual lifting of the depression beginning within several weeks of starting the medication. Some tricyclics are taken in three or four doses daily. Others are taken in a single dose because they act on the brain differently.

Unfortunately, in the process of increasing norepinephrine and serotonin levels, the cyclics tend to interfere with other neurotransmitter systems in the brain. Their action can lead to some unpleasant side effects, such as drowsiness, dizziness, and dry mouth. The side effects are dangerous when tricyclics are taken in too large a dose. These drugs may not be the best choice for individuals with certain additional psychological disorders, and people with alcohol abuse problems should avoid them, as well.

For many years, these drugs were the best available for fighting depression, and in some cases, they are still used. A physician or psychiatrist is aware of the medical conditions that may lead to problems with these medications and can help patients decide what is best for them.

## Monoamine Oxidase Inhibitors (MAOIs)

Another category of medications used to treat depression is the monoamine oxidase inhibitors (MAOIs). This group was discovered about the same time as imipramine, the first of the tricyclics. Drugs in this group were originally developed to treat tuberculosis, a lung disease. Psychiatrists became interested when they noticed an improvement in mood in some patients taking an MAOI for tuberculosis. Commmon MAOIs are Parnate (tranylcypromine), Nardil (phenelzine), and Marplan (isocarboxazid).

The MAOIs get their name from the fact that they act on, or inhibit, an enzyme called monoamine oxidase (MAO). An enzyme is a substance that causes a particular chemical action in the body. Monoamine oxidase is an enzyme that deactivates other amine enzymes, including the neurotransmitters serotonin, norepinephrine, and dopamine. So when monoamine oxidase is doing its job, levels of neurotransmitters are lower, and depression may be a result. MAO-inhibitor medications essentially stop monoamine oxidase from deactivating neurotransmitters, thus increasing neurotransmitter levels and providing relief from depression.

The problem is, besides having the undesirable effect of destroying the monoamine neurotransmitters, monoamine oxidase also works to eliminate another chemical called tyramine. This is a desirable effect, because tyramine raises blood pressure. When monoamine oxidase is inhibited, depression can be lifted, but blood levels of tyramine can rise, which causes blood pressure to rise. That can be dangerous.

When the MAO inhibitors were first developed, this side effect was unknown. When a number of cases of severe headaches due to a rise in blood pressure and even death from bleeding in the brain occurred in people taking MAO inhibitors, these drugs became unavailable in the United States for a number of years. Since then, they have been brought back because for some depressed people they seem to be the only medication that works. But now we know that people who take them need to be careful about what they eat and restrict their intake of foods that lead to a rise in tyramine. The interaction with some foods can even be deadly. Some of the foods that individuals taking MAOIs need to avoid include sausages, smoked meat, cheese, some kinds of fruit, coffee, chocolate, and soy sauce.

## A Prescription for Depression

Because of this, people who have trouble following a strict diet probably cannot take MAOIs. Individuals with high blood pressure, serious heart problems, or breathing problems related to bronchitis or asthma are not good candidates for these medications, either.

A newer type of MAOI is Emsam (selegiline). This medication works via a patch stuck to the skin, and it seems to cause fewer side effects than other MAOIs.

Balanced against the risks are certain notable benefits. "I've seen a few miracle cures with these drugs," one psychiatrist noted. "And they're particularly good if people suffer from panic attacks in addition to depression."[10]

**MAOIs can be effective in the treatment of depression, but they are not without risks. Those patients on MAOIs must keep away from certain foods, including chocolate, to avoid deadly reactions.**

## Norepinephrine and Dopamine Reuptake Inhibitors (NDRIs)

Wellbutrin (buprorion) is the one drug represented in this category. This med fights depression by targeting norepinephrine and dopamine levels. It doesn't cause some of the side effects of other antidepressants, but it does have one serious side effect of its own, and that is an increased risk of a seizure (a malfunctioning in the brain). On the benefit side, it is linked to fewer sexual side effects.[11]

## Serotonin and Norepinephrine Reuptake Inhibitors (SNRIs)

These a newer type of antidepressant. They block the reuptake of both serotonin and norepinephrine. They include Cymbalta (duloxetine), Effexor XR (venlafaxine), Pristiq, Khedezla (desvenlafaxine), and Fetzima (levomilnacipran).[12]

## Atypical Treatments

Some medications for depression don't fit neatly into a category. Effexor (venlafaxine) targets three neurotransmitters: norepinephrine, serotonin, and dopamine. Effexor is a reuptake inhibitor of serotonin and norepinephrine. Because it has a different chemical structure, some people who don't respond favorably to other antidepressants respond to Effexor.

Remeron (mirtazapine) has been around for about 20 years. It is prescribed for major depression and posttraumatic stress syndrome. In 2010, the FDA approved Oleptro (trazodone), which is known for its sleep-inducing qualities. In 2013, the FDA green-lighted Brintellix (vortioxetine) to treat adults with major depressive disorder.

*A Prescription for Depression*

## Sleeping Aids

When depression is associated with sleep problems, a doctor may prescribe sleep medications. Such drugs may provide temporary relief for difficulty sleeping, and they can sometimes significantly improve mood, especially when sleeplessness is a reaction to a particular worry or situation. But researchers note that sleeping pills are not likely to help either long-term sleep problems or the depression related to them.

## Herbal Therapy

For more than two thousand years, the herb St. John's wort (scientific name *Hypericum perforatum*) has been used for a variety of health purposes. Hippocrates of ancient Greece and Pliny of ancient Rome used it as a medicine. In the Middle Ages, St. John's wort was used to treat depression, and in the mid-nineteenth century, the Shakers, an American religious group known for their knowledge of herbs, used St. John's wort as a cure for "low spirits."[13]

St. John's wort has been studied through the years to try to discover the secrets of its healing powers. Those studies have found the plant to be generally safe, but some side effects may occur when St. John's wort is taken with certain medications, including some antidepressants. St. John's wort is very popular in Europe, particularly in Germany.

It appears that the part of the plant that gives it its reddish color is primarily responsible for St. John's wort's mood-boosting ability. This substance, hypericin, seems to interfere with the breakdown of neurotransmitters, acting in the same way as antidepressant medications.

The US National Institute of Mental Health led a study in which St. John's wort was compared with SSRIs in the treatment of depression. Patients with major depression were randomly assigned to one of three treatments: St. John's wort, an SSRI antidepressant, or a placebo. Although all three types of treatments helped some people, researchers were not able to prove that St. Johns' wort worked

*Are You Depressed?*

St. John's wort is one type of herbal therapy, which is an alternative to pharmaceutical treatment. St. John's wort is considered to be effective for the treatment of mild depression.

better than antidepressants or a placebo for major depression. (The antidepressant seemed to be slightly more effective by some measurements.) Still, those who believe in the effectiveness of St. John's wort say that, when used daily for a month or more, it helps mildly depressed people regain a more normal mood and attitude.[14] It is also sometimes used to help decrease the symptoms of mild anxiety and sleep disorders.

    A product called SAMe is a dietary supplement that is used in Europe to treat depression. The name is short for S-adenosyl–L-methionine, a chemical that occurs naturally in the body. Some scientists believe Omega-3 fatty acids, found in fish, walnuts and other foods, may relieve depression.[15]

# Mental Therapy and Beyond

While antidepressants and other medications may be prescribed for depression, the illness may be treated by addressing possible psychological causes. A person may have issues with negative thinking or low self-esteem that has sent them into a downward spiral. A person may be dealing with financial, relationship, or family problems. In these cases, psychological therapy may be more effective than any medicine. A person may have depression because of the way or habit of thinking that can be corrected by helping a person overcome these obstacles. Some depressed patients may not have a chemical balance that can be corrected with drugs. Others may need the counseling of mental therapy along with medication.

In cases in which depression seems to be a response to difficulties in life complicated by attitudes and behaviors that interfere with that individual's ability to cope, it makes sense that depression might be

*Are You Depressed?*

best treated by promoting changes in those attitudes and behaviors. Some researchers go so far as to say that even if a physical problem is the cause, a medical treatment might not be the best method. With drugs, recovery might be temporary and include side effects, while psychotherapy might prove more successful and longer lasting without side effects.

A person suffering from depression may need to see more than one kind of health care professional to get well. An individual may see a family doctor to rule out physical illness and perhaps to get started on medication. If the person sees a psychiatrist, that doctor may be able to provide a prescription for medication and monitor its use while also providing psychotherapy, or psychological treatment. Or the individual with depression may see a psychologist or some other type of counselor or therapist for psychological help. With the popularity of medical treatment for depression, it is easy to forget that, before the many medications that are available today were developed, almost all treatment for emotional and mental illness was psychological.

There is sometimes heated disagreement about which kind of treatment is best, with some people advocating only medical care (medication), while others believe only in psychological treatment (psychotherapy). Sometimes the best of both worlds comes together, and both medical and psychological treatments are used. Medication might be used first to improve a person's mood, and then psychotherapy might be tried to change underlying beliefs and behaviors. Various combinations of treatments receive widespread support. The bottom line is that no one treatment works for everyone. Just as there are many reasons people develop depression, there can be many pathways to getting well. And getting well is the ultimate goal.

## Psychological Treatment

Medical illness is something physically wrong in a living being. Mental or psychological illness is something wrong in the thinking

*Mental Therapy and Beyond*

**Members of group therapy can lend a sympathetic ear and provide suggestions based on their own experience. In addition, listening to the problems of others can put your own problems in perspective.**

or learning of a person. Psychotherapy treats psychological illness. Because depression can be caused by thinking or learning that produces behaviors that have negative results, psychotherapy can be an appropriate treatment. Psychotherapy aims to correct the thinking or learning that is causing problems.

Psychotherapy is also sometimes referred to as talk therapy or counseling. Psychotherapy can be described as a conversation between two people: an individual professionally trained to gather information in a particular way and a person seeking help.[1] Psychotherapy can strengthen a person's ability to cope with life's struggles. It can help a person understand the kinds of attitudes and behaviors that lead to depression.

Psychotherapists, or persons trained in psychotherapy, help patients understand how their past experiences contribute to their present attitudes and behaviors. They help patients to develop new coping skills and approach life's difficulties in more effective ways.

There are many forms of psychotherapy in use today. Many of them have their roots in psychoanalysis, the kind of psychotherapy developed by Sigmund Freud. Psychoanalysis involved the patient lying on a couch with the psychoanalyst sitting behind him or her while listening to the patient talk and helping the patient search through memories for thoughts and feelings developed in childhood that led to current problems. The patient would generally meet with the doctor three or four times a week for an hour each time over a period of years. As you can imagine, this treatment would get expensive, and results would take a long time. For those reasons, psychoanalysis is not a common treatment for depression today.

In the 1950s, Carl Rogers developed a new form of psychotherapy called client-centered therapy. This treatment focused on active listening. An active listener is focused on hearing what the individual is saying and truly understanding what he or she means. The person speaking, in this case an individual with depression, is directing the conversation as they explore their thoughts and feelings. Supporters of client-centered therapy believe that this technique can give the patient, as well as the doctor, a clearer understanding of the problems leading to depression.

## Changing Behavior

At about the same time that Carl Rogers was developing his active listening treatment, other researchers were developing a treatment called behavior therapy. Behavior therapy uses a variety of techniques to change behaviors that cause problems, such as the following:

*Relaxation training.* Learning how to relax the muscles of the body deeply has been proven to help reduce anxiety.

*Behavioral rehearsal.* This procedure helps the patient develop specific social skills. A therapist and patient put together a plan with steps that lead the patient toward a desired goal. The patient practices the steps until he or she can use the new behavior in everyday situations.

**Relabeling.** How a person responds to a situation emotionally is often the result of how the situation is labeled in the mind of that person. Behavior therapists help patients to become aware of how they think about situations. They encourage them to test their assumptions—things that are believed to be true without necessarily having evidence to support that belief—about situations that cause them severe stress.[2]

## Changing Negative Thoughts

Another form of psychological treatment is cognitive therapy. Cognition means thinking. Cognitive therapy is based on the idea that moods and emotions result from thought patterns. Cognitive therapy seeks to change a person's moods and emotions by changing that person's thinking.

Cognitive therapy was developed by Dr. Aaron Beck. Dr. Beck noticed that the patients who came to see him for depression all seemed to have overwhelmingly negative thoughts about themselves and life. He developed cognitive therapy as a way to treat depression by changing those negative thoughts. At about the same time, another psychologist, Albert Ellis, also developed an approach to psychotherapy that focused on cognition, or thoughts. Today a number of different forms of cognitive therapy are used to treat depression and other mood disorders.

Those who practice cognitive therapy are actively involved in the patient's treatment by asking for information and proposing possible solutions to problems. The cognitive therapist does not spend as much time looking into the past as is done in some other forms of therapy. The focus of cognitive therapy is the attitudes or assumptions individuals have about themselves and their place in the world that can lead to negative thoughts. It is these negative thoughts that are considered to be at the root of depression.[3]

*Are You Depressed?*

Cognitive therapy involves changing one's negative thought patterns. With careful work, patients can learn to replace negative thoughts with positive thoughts.

The therapist helps patients recognize their negative thoughts and see the problems caused by such thoughts. Once the patient sees the connection between these thoughts and the depressed feelings they have, they can begin to replace negative thoughts with appropriate, positive thoughts.

Some examples of the kinds of thinking errors targeted by cognitive therapy include such beliefs as: "I am of little value," "I am not capable of achieving anything of importance," or "Things are never going to change for the better." The first step for the cognitive therapist is to show the patient that these beliefs are not necessarily true; they are not based on reliable evidence. The next step is to change the patient's mistaken attitudes and replace them with more appropriate attitudes that can result in relief from depression.[4]

Cognitive and behavioral therapy are often now combined and called cognitive-behavior therapy, or CBT for short. Therapists who treat people with depression using CBT look at the ways in which people process and organize information about life. Depression is viewed as the outcome of mistaken negative beliefs. The goal of cognitive-behavior therapy is to replace negative thoughts and beliefs with more accurate and positive ones. Behavioral and cognitive techniques are used to accomplish this goal. Effective treatment involves working on the thinking, as well as the behaviors, that led to depression.

Many studies support the use of cognitive-behavior therapy with depressed patients. Some studies have compared the treatment of depression with CBT to treatment with antidepressant medication. One study done at the University of Toronto in Canada looked at what parts of the brain were affected by these treatments. Members of the CBT and the medication groups experienced about the same amount of improvement. Then the scientists scanned the patients' brains. "Our hypothesis was if you do well with treatment, your brain will have changed in the same way, no matter which treatment you received," said researcher Zindel Segal.[5]

But this was not the case. Patients' brains responded differently to the two kinds of treatment. CBT lowered activity in the part of the brain involved in reasoning and logic and raised activity in the brain's emotion center. Medication had the opposite effect. As another researcher, Helen Mayberg, explained, "Cognitive therapy targets the thinking brain, reshaping how you process information and changing your thinking pattern. It trains the brain to adopt different thinking circuits."[6]

Because CBT teaches new coping behaviors, it seems to retain its effect after treatment has ended. Some studies indicate that the changes brought about by CBT may be longer lasting than relief achieved through medication. One study went back a year after treatment to compare patients who had gone through cognitive therapy and patients who had taken medication. The researchers found that only about 31 percent of the cognitive therapy patients had relapsed, or had their depression return, after treatment was ended, while 76 percent of those who had taken medication relapsed once the medication stopped.[7]

Another plus for CBT is that it does not produce the side effects that are common with medications. Still, whether psychotherapy, such as CBT, can substitute for medical treatment is a subject of much disagreement. A more accepted belief is that antidepressant medications can work together with psychotherapy. For some patients, the relief of symptoms that can come with medication seems to be a necessary first step. As the depression begins to lift, patients may then be better able to participate in and benefit from psychotherapy.[8]

## Other Psychotherapy Methods

A number of other types of psychotherapy are also used to treat depression.

*Interpersonal therapy (IPT).* IPT focuses on improving personal relationships, especially relationships in which there are issues related to depression. During the first few sessions with an

IPT therapist, the patient and therapist discuss various relationships in the patient's life and identify issues, such as conflicts with family or friends, and the connection of those issues to the patient's depression. In the following sessions, usually over five or six months, these issues are worked on. According to the University of Michigan Depression Center, "Several years of careful study has shown that IPT is equally as effective in the short term treatment of depression as antidepressant medication therapy."[9] For the therapy to be even more effective, monthly follow-up sessions, called maintenance therapy, may be recommended.

***Additional therapies.*** Additional therapies are psychodynamic therapy and group therapy. In psychodynamic therapy, a therapist helps the patient try to resolve conflicts from the past to relieve depression. Group therapy uses feedback from a therapist and others who have experienced similar symptoms to ease depression. One of the key benefits of group therapy is that the patient sees that he or she is not alone; others have experienced depression and are working to overcome it.

***Electroconvulsive treatment (ECT).*** ECT, sometimes called electroshock therapy or simply shock therapy, is poorly understood by most people. Despite the scary images that may come to mind, ECT has been helpful to some people with depression. About one hundred thousand people are treated with ECT in the United States each year.[10]

In modern ECT, a controlled electric pulse is delivered through a padded electrode placed on the patient's head, which creates a brief electrical seizure. This seems to boost neurotransmitter levels in the brain, which is similar to the effect of antidepressant medications. The patient is given anesthesia beforehand so all muscles are relaxed, and the patient experiences none of the jumping or jerking that occurred with older methods. Some temporary memory loss may be experienced, especially for the time period right before the treatment, but significant permanent memory loss generally does not occur. Of the patients who fail to respond to drug treatment, approximately half respond to ECT.[11]

***Hospitalization.*** The kinds of therapies that have been looked at here are usually aimed at helping persons work through and get past their depression. But sometimes the symptoms interfere so much with life that the depressed person needs to be in a hospital where care can be given around the clock. Hospitalization may be critical when thoughts of suicide have been expressed. In a hospital setting, persons feeling suicidal can be watched carefully while they are being treated for depression.

***Bright lights.*** As we saw in Chapter 3, some people become depressed when there is not enough sunlight. Some people believe that the most effective treatment for this form of depression, known as seasonal affective disorder (SAD), is light therapy. This therapy involves sitting in front of special lights that are usually about ten times brighter than normal indoor light. Usually, this is only necessary in the wintertime, when shorter days bring on depression. The amount of time needed in front of the light can vary, but for some people, four to six hours of bright light each day is required. While sitting a few feet from the lights, patients can read, sew, or do paperwork as long as they keep their eyes open and glance directly into the light for a few seconds every minute or so. Although light therapy can be more time consuming than some other treatments and some researchers feel that evidence of its effectiveness is limited, it has few side effects.[12]

***Exercise.*** Some evidence suggests that regular aerobic exercise, such as running, biking, or swimming, can ease the symptoms of depression by raising the level of neurotransmitters in the brain in much the same way that antidepressants do. Even a brisk walk for ten to twenty minutes can help. A half-hour of exercise at a time at least three to five times a week seems to be one of the most effective for improving mood.

***Transcranial magnetic stimulation (TMS).*** This relatively new therapy is similar in some ways to electroconvulsive therapy (ECT),

*Mental Therapy and Beyond*

Exercise can help ease the symptoms of depression. An elevated heart rate raises the level of neurotransmitters in your brain. Exercises such as running, walking, and biking can also offer meditative benefits.

but it does not require anesthesia. This technique uses magnets to make nerve connections in the brain more efficient. Through a coil about the size of a human's hand held over the head of the patient, an electric current is generated in a targeted area of the brain. The electromagnet creates electric currents that stimulate nerve cells in the brain.

A small but growing number of patients have been treated with this method so far. It is an approach that patients may turn to when other therapies have failed. The benefits seem to last for around four months, at which time the treatment can be repeated. It may have fewer side effects than medications, but it is expensive because it requires a highly technical machine operated by a skilled technician. A variation on the treatment called deep TMS was approved by the FDA in 2013, and it has delivered a higher success rate than standard TMS. This therapy has advantages—it is not invasive and appears to have few side effects. Some have been pulled out of severe depression using this method.[13]

**Other alternative treatments.** Studies have been done on various alternative treatments for depression, including therapeutic writing intervention, massage, music therapy, and nutritional therapy. Additional studies are needed to further explore the effectiveness of these and other alternative treatments for depression.[14]

## Weighing the Options

The decision whether to choose medication, psychotherapy, ECT, some other treatment, or some combination of treatments depends on what kind of depression is involved, how much the depression is interfering with the individual's life, and a number of other factors. As author Anne Sheffield says in *How You Can Survive When They're Depressed*, "What works in one situation will not work in all; what may be useful in one case may be a waste of time and money in another, or in some instances downright dangerous."[15]

Here are some things to consider when deciding what kind of treatment to choose:

1. Some depressions will go away on their own over time. If living with depression is not causing too many problems at home, school, or work, medical or psychological treatment may not be necessary.
2. If a specific life event or a particular behavior seems to be the cause of the depression, psychotherapy may be a good treatment option.
3. Psychotherapy may also be a good choice when the person with depression has a tendency toward negative attitudes that a trained therapist can help with.
4. A form of depression called manic depression or bipolar disorder (which will be examined in the next chapter) should always be treated with medication.
5. Treatment costs and health insurance benefits may need to be considered when deciding on a form of treatment.[16]

# Conditions Related to Depression

Feelings of sadness, hopelessness, and distress may seem like depression, but they can be more than that. There are other psychological conditions or disorders that share some of the same symptoms with major depression, or unipolar disorder. Sometimes, a person may experience these illnesses along with their depression. For example, an individual may have both depression and an anxiety disorder. A medical professional can help diagnose if feelings of depression could be signs of other ailments. It's important to correctly identify an illness so the appropriate medications or other treatments can be applied.

## Dealing With Mania and Bipolar Disorder

As if severe depression were not bad enough, for some people it is only half the story. Some also experience extreme highs, called mania. For days or weeks, they feel on top of the world—as if nothing can stop them. That might sound good, but the problem is that they are out of touch with reality. They are hyperactive, they talk too loud and too fast, they spend money they do not have, and they think strangers—perhaps even dangerous ones—are their best friends. They engage in high-risk behaviors. They may become irritable or paranoid, and then suddenly, they crash and find themselves overwhelmed with hopelessness and guilt and swallowed up by depression.

This condition is called manic depression or bipolar disorder. It is called bipolar because of the two poles—periods of severe depression that alternate with periods of extreme or manic highs. Either of these states can be severe enough to require hospitalization to keep the individual from harming him- or herself. Persons with untreated bipolar disorder are likely to experience difficulties at school and work and in relationships. They may abuse alcohol or drugs. They may be at risk for suicide.

Bipolar disorder is not nearly as common as unipolar depression. Bipolar disorder affects approximately 5.7 million adult Americans, or about 2.6 percent of the US population, age eighteen and older every year, according to the National Institute of Mental Health. The average age for getting the condition is twenty-five.

Bipolar disorder is caused by a chemical imbalance in the brain. There is strong evidence that it is linked to genetics. An individual diagnosed with it often has family members with similar symptoms. More than two thirds of people with bipolar disorder have at least one close relative with the condition or with unipolar major depression.[1] This connection does not mean, however, that because one family member has this disorder, another family member definitely will. In at least some cases, certain life events can bring on the illness for which genetics has established a vulnerability.

Bipolar disorder is considered a lifelong illness to be treated rather than cured. Statistics indicate that 90 percent of those who experience both the extreme lows and the extreme highs of bipolar disorder need continued treatment for this illness. It seems to

*Conditions Related to Depression*

Bipolar disorder is characterized by manic episodes. People who suffer from bipolar disorder are often said to have high highs and low lows.

strike young men and women with equal frequency. Children and teenagers younger than twenty who have had episodes of major depression may be at increased risk for developing bipolar disorder.[2]

The good news is that effective treatments are available, and with treatment, individuals with bipolar disorder can channel their talents and abilities into productive lives. Actress Patty Duke struggled with bipolar disorder for many years before finding the treatment that would allow her to enjoy the success her hard work had earned. Dr. Kay Redfield Jamison is a highly successful psychiatrist who has used all she learned about her own manic depression to help others understand this disorder.

Three main types of medication are used to treat bipolar disorder: mood stabilizers, such as lithium; anticonvulsants, such as carbamazepine, which help stop intense muscle contractions; and antipsychotic medications, such as thioridazine, which help an individual stay in touch with reality.[3]

The drug that has been used the longest for bipolar disorder is lithium. It is a mineral that is present in some soils. The early Greeks noticed that when people with what they called melancholy bathed in spring water that contained a lot of lithium salts, they became happier.

Today, lithium is used mostly to even out the mountains and valleys of a person's emotional swings. It can bring someone down from mania and control mood in some people. Sometimes an antidepressant is also prescribed to deal with the lows, but the drug has to be carefully monitored so it doesn't bring on rapid changes in moods.

People on lithium need to have their blood levels tested regularly because lithium only works when it is at the right level in the bloodstream, and the difference between the right amount and enough to make a person sick is quite small. Alcohol can cause problems and should be avoided by people taking lithium.

In recent years, a number of new medications have been introduced to treat bipolar disorder, including Depakene (valproic acid), Depakote (divalproex sodium), Tegretol and Equetro (carbamazepine), and Lamictal (lamotrigine). Some of these medications are now used instead of lithium or in combination with it. If mania and depression continue after trying any of these drugs, doctors many prescribe antipsychotic medication. The medication Symbyax combines the antidepressant fluoxetine with the antipsychotic olanzapine. The Mayo Clinic says that it works as a depression treatment and a mood stabilizer. Approved by the FDA, Symbyax is designed specifically for the treatment of depressive episodes associated with bipolar disorder.[4]

These medications are an important part of the treatment of bipolar disorder. For many years, lithium seemed to be the only choice, and if it did not work, there were few alternatives. But since these drugs are fairly new, we don't know if people who do well on them at first will continue to see that improvement after the many years of treatment that bipolar disorder requires. Only time will tell.

## Coping With High Anxiety

Anxiety is a normal reaction to stress. It helps people deal with challenges and work through problems. But when anxiety becomes extreme, dealing with those same problems becomes difficult. Then anxiety becomes a disorder.

Many studies have found that depression and anxiety disorders often occur together. In fact, statistics suggest that nearly half the people who suffer from depression also have some type of anxiety disorder.[5] Sometimes the anxiety episodes only happen when depression is present, and sometimes the two problems occur separately and follow different paths. Research continues to search out the connections between these disorders.

The sidebar on the next page shows some of the types of anxiety disorders identified by the *DSM-5*. An individual with a panic disorder might have a sudden feeling that something terrible is about to happen, along with such physical symptoms as a rapid heartbeat, difficulty catching one's breath, dizziness, weakness,

*Are You Depressed?*

## Types of Anxiety Disorders

- Panic disorder
- Agoraphobia
- Social phobia
- Obsessive-compulsive disorder (OCD)
- Posttraumatic stress disorder (PTSD)
- Generalized anxiety disorder (GAD)

sweating, choking, nausea, and a tingling feeling. A panic attack can happen at any time and take an individual completely by surprise. In fact, some people have experienced panic attacks in their sleep!

A phobia is an intense fear of something that is not obviously frightening to most people. Agoraphobia is described as a fear of being in situations from which escape could be difficult or embarrassing. The dictionary defines it as an abnormal fear of being in crowds, public places, or open areas. It is a kind of anxiety disorder. Sometimes agoraphobia develops when a panic disorder is not effectively treated.

Social phobia, also called social anxiety disorder, occurs when individuals find themselves overwhelmed with anxiety in certain situations around other people. A particular kind of situation, such as eating with others, may cause trouble, or people with social phobia may have difficulty just about any time they are in public. These situations might bring on such symptoms as an upset stomach, sweating, blushing, trembling, or difficulty speaking.

People who are diagnosed with obsessive-compulsive disorder (OCD) have repeated unwanted thoughts, or obsessions, along with repeated behaviors, or compulsions. The repeated behaviors, such as frequent hand washing, may be related to the unwanted thoughts, such as an excessive concern about germs.

Posttraumatic stress disorder is that grouping of symptoms that tends to appear after an intensely negative or shocking life event. We most commonly hear about PTSD in relation to soldiers who have been in combat. It can also result from a bad accident, an attack, or a natural disaster. Persons with PTSD may experience frightening thoughts about the traumatic event, difficulty sleeping, jumpiness, uneasiness, or feelings of emotional numbness.

It is estimated that about 3 percent of Americans have generalized anxiety disorder (GAD). It affects 6.8 million adults. Women are twice as likely to be affected as men..[6] This disorder is defined by continuous, exaggerated worry that the individual cannot shake. These tense, worried feelings are often accompanied by tiredness, headache, muscle aches, sweating, and crabbiness.

Avoidance behavior, such as staying in bed for long periods of time and avoiding activities that used to be fun, is often seen in persons with anxiety disorder. By shutting down, the individual is avoiding the pain.

A link between depression and anxiety disorders has been suspected since at least the 1960s, when researchers noticed that some patients with severe anxiety symptoms seemed less anxious after being given antidepressants.[7] This treatment seemed to be most effective in patients who had attacks of anxiety separated by periods of much less anxiety rather than in those who were continuously anxious.

Anxiety disorders are treatable, but only about one third of those suffering receive treatment.[8] Psychotherapy can be an important part of the treatment for an anxiety disorder. As might be expected, when people with this disorder come up against a situation that causes them problems, anxiety begins to rise. Studies show that if the individual is able to stay in contact with the feared situation in a safe environment for long enough, the anxiety level reaches a peak

## Are You Depressed?

Some phobias can be psychologically disabling if gone untreated. Agoraphobics avoid crowds, enclosed spaces, and potentially embarrassing situations.

and then begins to decrease. Skilled psychotherapists help their patients face the fear and work through it.

Often, medications used to treat depression can help anxiety, such as selective serotonin reuptake inhibitors, serotonin-norepinephrine reuptake inhibitors, and tricyclic antidepressants. A class of drug called benzodiazepines is often used for short-term anxiety management. The medications include alprazolam, clonazepam, diazepam, and lorazepam. They help promote relaxation, reduce muscular tension, and relieve other physical symptoms of anxiety.[9]

## Borderline Personality Disorder

Borderline personality disorder (BPD) is a mental disorder involving extremely intense and changeable moods and emotions. Persons with BPD tend to experience intense episodes of anger, depression, and anxiety that may appear suddenly and may be accompanied by aggression toward others, acts of self-injury, or drug or alcohol abuse. They may have difficulty getting along with others, but at the same time, they may frantically try to avoid being alone.

It is believed that about 1.6 percent of adults have BPD, although some estimate that almost 6 percent may have it. It is more common in women than men. About three quarters of cases are women. It often occurs together with other psychiatric problems, including major or unipolar depression, bipolar disorder, and anxiety disorders. Treatment often includes some form of psychotherapy to work on behaviors associated with this illness. Sometimes medications are prescribed to target specific symptoms. Research continues to try to understand the brain chemistry and environmental triggers that lead to BPD and to help the individuals who suffer from it lead normal, productive lives.[10]

## When Alcohol and Drugs are in the Mix

Just as major depression and anxiety disorders can occur together, major depression and chemical dependency can go hand in hand, as well. Some people with mood disorders drink excessively or use other substances that bring on a high or euphoria because the chemicals temporarily relieve the pain of depression. Often, however, such efforts to treat mood problems with drugs or alcohol set another chain of events in motion that can lead to still more problems.

Because chemical dependency can cause some of the same symptoms as depression, and depression can look a lot like chemical dependency, it can be difficult to be sure which is the root of the problem in a particular case. A leading expert on alcoholism has stated that in about 90 percent of patients who have symptoms of both alcoholism and depression, the depression is secondary to the alcoholism.[11] Sorting out the cause and effect can be an important step in getting the right treatment.

# 7

# Getting Help

Depression not only affects the millions who have the condition, it affects millions of the friends, families, and associates who know the depressed. Those who live or work with someone who is depressed can also suffer. They may feel confused, demoralized, doubting, or resentful. Ann Sheffield, who authored the book *How You Can Survive When They're Depressed*, calls the phenomenon "depression fallout." It especially affects the people closest to those who have the illness—spouses, parents, and children. These are the people who "experience the consequences of living in close proximity to someone else's despair."[1]

One father whose daughter had severe depression described it as "being part of a funeral that never ends."[2]

In *Overcoming Depression*, authors Dr. Demitri F. Papolos and Janice Papolos state:

*When a relative experiences repeated episodes of depression or mania, there is an extremely disruptive and disorganizing effect on family life. The other members of the family are faced with the challenge of looking after and providing for the needs of their relative while at the same time maintaining their other responsibilities at work and at home—often within an atmosphere of confusion, isolation, embarrassment, anger, and guilt.*[3]

## Family Ties

When the person with depression is a child, parents suffer along with their child; they are likely to wonder what the child's future will be like. Under such circumstances, the needs of other family members often go unmet.

When a family member is depressed, other family members may feel that giving that person extra attention will make him or her feel better. When the depressed person does not respond positively to attention, other family members are likely to feel frustrated, angry, or guilty. These feelings can lead to a cycle of exhaustion and negative emotions for everyone involved.

While each family's story is unique, common problems and emotions tend to arise repeatedly. With professional help, families can learn ways to cope.

The first task for each family member is to understand depression. The idea of mental illness and the vocabulary of psychiatry and medications can be confusing and even frightening—for the person with depression and for family and friends. An individual with depression can greatly benefit from an ally, or someone to provide support, guidance, and understanding throughout treatment. As Dr. Francis Mark Mondimore says, "What patients do not need is someone telling them to 'shape up' or 'snap out of it,' as if that's all it takes to get better. What they do need is someone who can help them get help."[4]

A fairly common misconception is that people with depression should be able to cheer up and talk themselves out of it on their

*Getting Help*

Parents of depressed children often feel guilty for passing on a genetic disposition to depression. Depression can take a toll on the family in many ways.

own. According to a survey by the Alliance for the Mentally Ill of Pennsylvania, 40 percent of those surveyed believed that "most people who are mentally ill could be well if they only had the will."[5] In another poll, this one by the National Institute of Mental Health, about half the people surveyed felt that depression was a "personal weakness" rather than a health problem.[6]

Actually, just the opposite is often true. Many people with depression demonstrate a great deal of strength in the face of their illness. As a social scientist who also suffers from depression, David Karp wrote in *Speaking of Sadness*, "Each interview caused me to marvel at the courage depressed people display in dealing with extraordinary pain."[7]

Whether we think of depression as a physical illness or a psychological disorder, it is not just a personal weakness someone should be able to get over without help. Everyone struggles to overcome the ordinary, occasional feelings of being depressed, especially as a result of one of life's many setbacks. Hardly ever can full-blown major depression be conquered alone. That is not to say that it cannot be conquered—it means that professional help can make a huge difference.

As the author of *Depression, the Mood Disease* says, "People who are suffering from mood disorders need a tremendous amount of professional support, reassurance, and education."[8] Especially at the beginning of treatment, frequent visits to a health care professional may be needed. It takes time and help to get well.

Another important factor in overcoming illness is a positive attitude and a belief that help is available and treatment will work. Unfortunately, a person suffering from major depression may find a positive attitude extremely difficult if not impossible. Hopelessness is a symptom of the illness, and efforts to get well can seem wasted and pointless.

"This is where family and friends come in," says author Dr. Francis Mark Mondimore. "They must be the source of support and optimism in treatment. I sometimes tell family members who wonder why their relative is so complaining and rejecting that it's the illness talking. It's important to remember that this attitude will disappear when the illness is successfully treated. To criticize the depressed person for resisting treatment is like blaming someone with a broken leg for not being able to walk."[9]

Sometimes people with depression lack the energy to seek help. Worse still is the fear that their depression is their own fault and others will blame them for how they feel. Sadly, this can be true if family and friends do not understand depression. Too many depressed people do not get help for their disorder; they fear the label of mental illness so much that they try to hide and live with their pain. In an article in *The American Journal of Managed Care*, Aron Halfin, MD, reports that "depression remains a significantly underrecognized and undertreated condition with less than one third of adults with depression obtaining appropriate professional treatment."[10] This is due to several factors, including cost and availability of appropriate care, and something called stigma.

## Overcoming Public Perception

One of the problems that sufferers of depression face is the stigma of mental illness. Stigma is a negative meaning or attitude attached to something. Former First Lady Rosalynn Carter, who has worked hard on behalf of mental health care, describes stigma as "the tremendous gap between what the experts know about brain-related illnesses and what the public understands."[11] Because there is so much misunderstanding about brain-related illnesses, people who seek help often face discrimination in what schools they can attend, what jobs they can get, what kind of health care benefits they can receive, and much more. Such discrimination is the result of stigma.

"Stigma breeds shame and silence where neither should exist," says author Anne Sheffield. "There is nothing shameful about mental illness; an illness is an illness, whether of the brain, the heart, or the lung."[12]

People with mental illness are often feared. While some individuals with mental illness are capable of doing harm to themselves or others, according to the American Psychiatric Association, people with mental illness, like other people with disabilities, are far more likely to be victims of crime than they are to be criminals.[13]

One form of discrimination is a lack of medical insurance coverage for psychiatric benefits. As difficult as it can be to get affordable health care for physical illness, the costs and other difficulties can be many times magnified for mental illness. Rosalynn Carter says, "I firmly believe that making insurance benefits for mental illnesses and physical illnesses the same would do more than anything to dispel stigma."[14]

Mental health care is generally treated differently by insurance companies than physical health care.[15] Office visits to a psychiatrist or counselor may be limited or not covered at all, and the portion of the bill paid by the insurance company may be lower. Insurance companies often place a strict limit on the number of days a patient can stay in a psychiatric hospital, and this limit can be well under the amount of time needed to get well. Mental health organizations are working to pass laws to correct this situation, but today, the lack of insurance coverage is a serious problem for many people seeking treatment.

## When It Feels Like There's No Way Back

Few who have not experienced it understand just how terrible the pain of major depression can truly be. Mike Wallace, a former anchor of the CBS television news program *60 Minutes*, writes:

> It's difficult to make others understand how desperate a deep depression can make you feel, how lost, how cope-less, how grim. And no light at the end of the tunnel. And there is no way properly to describe the anguish that a depressive can put his family through. Gloom, doom, no love, no real communication, short temper, and leave-me-alone fault-finding.[16]

## Getting Help

This terrible pain brings us to the most serious consequence of untreated or ineffectively treated major depression—the risk of suicide.

Statistics vary because some suicides may be misreported as accidents, and families may want to remain silent about such a tragic event. In 2013, there were 41,149 deaths by suicide in the US. Suicide is the tenth leading cause of death in the country. It is the second leading cause of death for fifteen to twenty-four year olds, preceded only by accidents.[17] Author Anne Sheffield writes that probably 90 percent of those teenagers suffered from some form of depression or other psychiatric disorder, and many also had drug and alcohol problems.[18]

In a *New York Times* interview after a young person committed suicide, Dr. Thomas Jensen, the head of the adolescent psychiatric unit of St. Mary's Hospital in Lewiston, Maine, said, "When you are depressed, you could have a million things going for you but if one

## Know the Suicide Warning Signs

The following are potential signs that a person may take his or her life. Knowing these signs could help you save a life.

- Talk of suicide
- Constant thoughts of and talk about hopelessness and death
- Increased risk taking
- Withdrawal
- A new crisis for someone who was already depressed
- Sudden change in attitude, such as sudden calm after prolonged depression
- Putting things in order or tying things up

thing is wrong, the depressed person completely loses perspective. He focuses on that one negative thing, and he convinces himself that suicide is the only option." A boy who had thought about suicide while depressed reported later, "My God, I was so distorted. It was scary. I look back now and think, 'How could I have even thought of killing myself?' But I thought it was the only option. I know better now."[19]

Ironically, there are steps in the process of getting help for depression that can increase the risk of suicide. Sometimes severely depressed people are so withdrawn that any action, even suicide, is too much of an effort. As they begin to get better and begin to have more energy but are still a long way from well, they may have enough energy but not enough hope, and they may try to take their life.

Another frightening irony is that some studies indicate an increased risk for suicide among people taking antidepressants. These results remain controversial, but manufacturers of antidepressants are required to include a warning about the increased risk of suicide or suicidal thinking for children or adolescents when taking these drugs.

## Know the Risk Factors for Teen Suicide

Warning signs for teenage suicide include the following:

- People who have made previous attempts at suicide may try again, especially during the first months after an unsuccessful attempt.
- Teens who have been hospitalized for psychiatric care have an increased risk of suicide.
- Teens who talk of being a failure and see themselves as unable to meet the high standards of themselves or others may be at risk for suicide.
- A recent loss may leave a vulnerable teenager so lost and alone that suicide seems to be the only option.

Getting Help

- Some teens abuse drugs or alcohol to deal with the pain of depression, and this combination can increase the chances of a suicide attempt.
- A gun in the house may make it easy for a troubled teen to commit suicide. According to teen suicide expert Dr. Richard O'Connor, "If you have a gun in your home, you are five times more likely to have a suicide in your house than homes without a gun."[20]
- Young people who come from families that regularly resolve conflict through violence may be at greater risk of using violence against themselves.
- Teens who have never learned the communication skills that allow for a discussion of their feelings may turn to suicide.[21]

The bottom line—if a person is feeling too low to enjoy life and these feelings keep hanging on for weeks at a time, that person should get help. Thoughts of suicide mean it is crucial to get help right away.

## How to Take Action to Prevent Suicide

If someone you know exhibits suicide warning signs:

- Remove access to weapons
- Remove access to medications that could be harmful in overdose
- Keep the lines of communication open, especially avoiding giving the depressed person reason to put him- or herself down even more

If you are having thoughts of suicide:

- Call a suicide hotline or 911
- Go to an emergency room
- Tell someone you know will help you to get help

*Are You Depressed?*

Often, patients undergoing treatment for depression are at risk for suicide. It is important to eliminate any high risk factors, such as the availibility of guns.

*Getting Help*

If a friend or family member confesses thoughts of suicide to you, always take the matter seriously. Tell someone who can help.

## Steps to Getting Better

It has been said that one of the best ways to prevent suicide is to prevent the return of depression. Getting effective treatment and working until the depressed person truly feels better need to be priorities.

"There are two parts to the equation: a skilled doctor and a patient who realizes that he or she also shapes the outcome of treatment," say the authors of *Overcoming Depression*. "Success very much depends on the ability of the patient to take an active part in and make a commitment to the treatment alliance."[22]

If medication is tried, the patient has to understand and accept that a period of trial-and-error can take months. If one medication does not work, time will be needed for it to clear from the patient's system before another is tried. This time of uncertainty, which may last months or even years, can be very frustrating, and the patient may become angry and may find it difficult to be hopeful.

Sometimes patients turn their negative feelings against the professionals who are trying to help them. Depressed people may stop taking the medications prescribed for them or change the amount or timing of taking medications without consulting a doctor. They may have unrealistic expectations of the doctor or therapist, and they may become disappointed or angry when their expectations are not met. They may continually miss appointments and give up on treatment.[23]

This is why it is so important for the individual with depression to recognize the choices that he or she needs to make to get well. Otherwise, as one patient puts it, "It makes it too easy for patients to take themselves off the hook of personal responsibility and to behave like victims, which is not healthy in the long run. I see it as similar to taking insulin for diabetes and then ignoring the need for an appropriate diet."[24]

Sarah Carlisle is a therapist who understands living with depression because she has the disorder herself. Carlisle knows how important it is to take her physical and emotional health needs seriously. She deals with her depression through medication, psychiatric care, yoga, and personal relationships—a combination that allows her to be successful. For her, a red flag to watch for is loss of appetite. "That's my cue that I need to pay extra attention to taking care of myself and see my doctor if it doesn't get better. I may not ever be cured, but proper treatment keeps me feeling happy and healthy, emotionally and physically."[25]

## Help From Professional Organizations

A number of organizations can help with gaining understanding and getting help. The National Depressive and Manic Depressive Association (NDMDA) provides support and encouragement to patients and their families through support groups and educational programs. NDMDA publishes a newsletter with information about new treatments and sponsors conventions and workshops. Upon request, the NDMDA will send a list of available resources.

## Strategies for Self-Help

Sometimes, taking some simple measures can help decrease the symptoms of depression. People experiencing depression may try the following:

- Get enough sleep
- Eat a healthy diet
- Find ways to relax
- Get involved in activities you enjoy or used to enjoy even when you don't really feel like doing anything
- Seek help at times when you feel low or face extra stress

## Sleep Tips

Sleeplessness can add to depression and be caused by depression. Getting rest can help relieve symptoms. Here are a few suggestions for getting a good night's sleep.

- Go to bed and get up at about the same time every day
- Don't take afternoon naps if you have trouble falling asleep at night
- Do something relaxing before bed
- Get some exercise every day
- Avoid caffeine and alcohol
- Avoid large meals and beverages late at night

The National Alliance for the Mentally Ill (NAMI) started in 1979, and it has since grown into a nationwide organization with chapters in every state. NAMI members work for better access to mental health services and insurance benefits for everyone affected by mental illness. They also seek to educate family members of mental health patients and the general public about psychiatric issues.

The National Mental Health Association is another national organization with chapters all over the country. It is an excellent resource for learning about mental health issues.

## Reasons to be Positive

At this time, there is no cure for depression, but there are many ways to deal with and control the disorder. According to former First Lady Rosalynn Carter:

> *Depression is the most treatable of all the mental illnesses. With our new knowledge of the brain, diagnoses are more accurate and treatments have improved considerably, bringing relief to many*

If you or someone you know is contemplating suicide, it is vital to reach out for help. There are many resources available that will help you manage this most treatable of mental illnesses.

*who have suffered. If you or someone you care about is having symptoms that you think may be the result of depression, you should seek help from a mental health professional. There is no need to suffer unnecessarily when there is so much help available.*[26]

New and better treatments for mood disorders will continue to become available. Better medications will be developed with fewer side effects. Treatments that involve such natural therapies as light, sleep, nutrition, and exercise will become more effective and reduce the need for medication. Advanced technologies for looking into the brain may help in understanding, diagnosing, and treating depression.

The actress Patty Duke also reminds those with depression to be patient and give it some time, "My recovery Catherine Zeta Jones from manic depression has been an evolution, not a sudden miracle."[27]

The TV news journalist Jane Pauley has suffered from depression and she offers encouraging words for those who may also have the illness: "I didn't suffer the misconception that depression was all in my head of a mark of poor character. I knew it was a disease, and like all diseases, was treatable."[28]

# Chapter Notes

## Chapter 1: Into the Bleak

1. "Kevin Breel: Confessions of a Depressed Comic," TED, May 2013, <http://www.ted.com/talks/kevin_breel_confessions_of_a_depressed_comic?language=en> (April 8, 2015).
2. Michael Friedman, "Why Robin Williams Lost to Depression," CNN, August 13, 2014, < http://www.cnn.com/2014/08/13/opinion/friedman-robin-williams/> (April 8, 2015).
3. "Major Depression Among Adults," National Institute of Mental Health, <http://www.nimh.nih.gov/health/statistics/prevalence/major-depression-among-adults.shtml > (April 8, 2015).
4. "Workplace Health Promotion: Depression," Centers for Disease Control and Prevention. Last updated October 23, 2013, <http://www.cdc.gov/workplacehealthpromotion/implementation/topics/depression.html > (April 8, 2015).
5. "Depression Can Break Your Heart," MedicineNet.com, <http://www.medicinenet.com/script/main/art.asp?articlekey=21761> (April 8, 2015).
6. Peter Wehrwein, "Astounding increase in antidepressant use by Americans," *Harvard Health Blog*, October 20, 2011, <http://www.health.harvard.edu/blog/astounding-increase-in-antidepressant-use-by-americans-201110203624> (April 8, 2015).
7. Carol Turkington and Eliot F. Kaplan, *Making the Antidepressant Decision* (Chicago, Ill.: Contemporary Books, 2001), p. 46.

*Are You Depressed?*

8. Siddhartha Mukherjee, "Post-Prozac Nation," *The New York Times Magazine*, April 19, 2012, < http://www.nytimes.com/2012/04/22/magazine/the-science-and-history-of-treating-depression.html > (April 8, 2015).
9. Margarita Tartakovsky, "Depression: New Medications on the Horizon," *PsychCentral*, < http://psychcentral.com/lib/depression-new-medications-on-the-horizon/0005794> (April 8, 2015).
10. <http://www.dsm5.org/Pages/Default.aspx>.

## Chapter 2: Recognizing the Signs

1. David A. Karp, *Speaking of Sadness: Depression, Disconnection, and the Meanings of Illness* (New York, N.Y.: Oxford University Press, 1996), p. 3.
2. Demitri F. Papolos and Janice Papolos, *Overcoming Depression* (New York, N..Y.: Harper & Row Publishers, 1987), p. 10.
3. Carol Turkington and Eliot F. Kaplan, *Making the Antidepressant Decision* (Chicago, Ill.: Contemporary Books, 2001), p. xxi.
4. "Major Depression Among Adults," National Institute of Mental Health, <http://www.nimh.nih.gov/health/statistics/prevalence/major-depression-among-adults.shtml> (April 8, 2015).
5. Ginny Graves, "The Hidden Signs of Depression," *Self*, February 2007, p. 99.
6. "Criteria for Major Depressive Episode: DSM-5," National Alliance on Mental Illness, <http://www2.nami.org/Content/NavigationMenu/Intranet/Homefront/Criteria_Major_D_Episode.pdf > (April 8, 2015).
7. "One in 40 Infants Experience Baby Blues, Doctors Say," *ABC News*, November 9, 2006, <http://abcnews.go.com/Health/OnCall/story?id=2640591 > (April 8, 2015).

8. Joan L. Luby, et.al, "The clinical significance of preschool depression: Impairment in functioning and clinical markers of the disorder," *Journal of Affective Disorders*, January 2009, <http://www.ncbi.nlm.nih.gov/pmc/articles/PMC2587510/> (April 8, 2015).

9. Ralph E. Cash, "Depression in Young Children: Information for Parents and Educators," National Association of School Psychologists, 2004, <http://www.nasponline.org/communications/spawareness/depressyc_ho.pdf> (April 8, 2015).

10. Depression in Children and Adolescents Fact Sheet, National Alliance on Mental Illness, Reviewed July 2010, <http://www2.nami.org/Content/ContentGroups/Illnesses/Depression_in_Children_and_Adolescents.htm> (April 8, 2015).

11. Women and Depression Fact Sheet, National Alliance on Mental Illness, Reviewed October 2009, <http://www2.nami.org/Content/NavigationMenu/Mental_Illnesses/Women_and_Depression/womenanddepression.pdf > (April 8, 2015).

12. "Depression is Not a Normal Part of Growing Old," Centers for Disease Control and Prevention, Reviewed May 2, 2012, <http://www.cdc.gov/aging/mentalhealth/depression.htm>.

## Chapter 3: The Root of the Blues

1. Stephanie Burcusa, "Risk of Recurrence in Depression," *Clinical Psychology Review*, December 2007, <http://www.ncbi.nlm.nih.gov/pmc/articles/PMC2169519/> (April 8, 2015).

2. "Major Depression and Genetics," Stanford School of Medicine, <http://depressiongenetics.stanford.edu/mddandgenes.html> (April 8, 2015).

3. Gerome Breen, et. al., "A Genome-Wide Significant Linkage for Severe Depression on Chromosome 3: The Depression

Network Study," *The American Journal of Psychaiatry*, August 2011. <http://ajp.psychiatryonline.org/doi/abs/10.1176/appi.ajp.2011.10091342> (April 8, 2015).

4. Heather A. Turner and Melissa J. Butler, "Direct and Indirect Effects of Childhood Adversity on Depressive Symptoms in Young Adults," *Journal of Youth and Adolescence* (2003), vol. 32, iss. 2, p. 89.

5. Ibid., p. 3.

6. Allan M. Leventhal and Christopher R. Martell, *The Myth of Depression as Disease* (Westport, Conn.: Praeger Publishers, 2006), p. 69.

7. Mondimore, p. 75.

8. "Insufficient Sleep Is a Public Health Epidemic," Centers for Disease Control and Prevention, reviewed January 13, 2014, <http://www.cdc.gov/features/dssleep/> (April 8, 2015).

9. "Depression and Sleep," National Sleep Foundation, 2007, <http://www.sleepfoundation.org/site/apps/nlnet/content3.aspx?c=huIXKjM0IxF&b=2427705&content_id={90A2192C-A80E-467B-85AD-25CA3EE85356}&notoc=1> (August 21, 2008).

10. "Seasonal Affective Disorder," *Psychology Today*, November 24, 2014, <https://www.psychologytoday.com/conditions/seasonal-affective-disorder> (April 8, 2015).

11. Francis Mark Mondimore, *Depression, the Mood Disease* (Baltiimore, Md.: The Johns Hopkins Univeristy Press, 1993), p. 168.

## Chapter 4: A Prescription for Depression

1. "Depression," National Alliance on Mental Illness, Reviewed October 2009, <http://www2.nami.org/Template.cfm?Section=Depression&Template=/ContentManagement/ContentDisplay.cfm&ContentID=87942> (April 8, 2015).

## Chapter Notes

2. Mark A. Reinecke and Michael R. Davison, eds., *Comparative Treatments of Depression* (New York, N.Y.: Springer Publishing Company, 2002), p. xii.
3. Turkington and Kaplan, p. 58.
4. Francis Mark Mondimore, *Depression, the Mood Disease* (Baltimore, Md.: Johns Hopkins University Press, 1993), p. 57.
5. Lisa L. Weyandt, *The Physiological Basis of Cognitive and Behavioral Disorders* (Mahwah, N. J.: Lawrence Erlbaum Associates, 2006), p. 150.
6. Allan M. Leventhal and Christopher R. Martell, *The Myth of Depression as Disease* (Westport, Conn.: Praeger Publishers, 2006), p. 33.
7. "Pharmaceutical Sales 2010," Drugs.com <http://www.drugs.com/top200_units.html> (April 8, 2015).
8. Turkington and Kaplan, p. 63.
9. "Depression (major depressive disorder)," Mayo Clinic <http://www.mayoclinic.org/diseases-conditions/depression/in-depth/antidepressants/art-20046273> (April 8, 2015).
10. Turkington and Kaplan,., p. 170.
11. "Antidepressants: Selecting one that's right for you," Mayo Clinic, <http://www.mayoclinic.org/diseases-conditions/depression/in-depth/antidepressants/art-20046273> (April 8, 2015).
12. Ibid.
13. Turkington and Kaplan, p. 201.
14. Ibid., p. 202.
15. "Depression (major depression): Alternative Medicine," Mayo Clinic, <http://www.mayoclinic.org/diseases-conditions/depression/basics/alternative-medicine/con-20032977> (April 8, 2015).

## Chapter 5: Mental Therapy and Beyond

1. Demitri F. Papolos and Janice Papolos, *Overcoming Depression* (New York, N.Y.: Harper & Row Publishers, 1987), p. 140.
2. Allan M. Leventhal and Christopher R. Martell, *The Myth of Depression as Disease* (Westport, Conn.: Praeger Publishers, 2006), p. 123.
3. Francis Mark Mondimore, *Depression, the Mood Disease* (Baltimore, Md.: Johns Hopkins University Press, 1993), p. 208.
4. Anne Sheffield, *How You Can Survive When They're Depressed* (New York, N.Y.: Three Rivers Press, 1998), p. 113.
5. Sharon Begley, "How the Brain Rewires Itself," *Time*, January 29, 2007, p. 77.
6. Ibid., p. 78.
7. Leventhal and Martell, p. 124.
8. Carol Turkington and Eliot F. Kaplan, *Making the Antidepressant Decision* (Chicago, Ill.: Contemporary Books, 2001), p. xv.
9. "Interpersonal Psychotherapy for Depression," University of Michigan Depression Center, 2003–2006, <http://www.med.umich.edu/depression/ipt.htm> (August 22, 2008).
10. Turkington and Kaplan, p. 46.
11. Sheffield, p. 96.
12. Mondimore, p. 145.
13. Roni Caryn Rabin, "New Approach to Depression," *The New York Times*, July 1, 2013, <http://well.blogs.nytimes.com/2013/07/01/new-approach-to-depression/?_r=0> (April 8, 2015).
14. Lisa L. Weyandt, *The Physiological Basis of Cognitive and Behavioral Disorders* (Mahwah, N. J.: Lawrence Erlbaum Associates, 2006), p. 158.

15. Sheffield, p. 101.
16. Ibid., p. 114.

## Chapter 6: Conditions Related to Depression

1. "Bipolar Disorder Statistics," Depression and Bipolar Support Alliance, <http://www.dbsalliance.org/site/PageServer?pagename=education_statistics_bipolar_disorder> (April 8, 2015).
2. Lisa L. Weyandt, *The Physiological Basis of Cognitive and Behavioral Disorders* (Mahwah, N. J.: Lawrence Erlbaum Associates, 2006), p. 161.
3. Ibid., p. 172.
4. "Bipolar disorder: Treatment and drugs," Mayo Clinic, <http://www.mayoclinic.org/diseases-conditions/bipolar-disorder/basics/treatment/con-20027544> (April 8, 2015).
5. "Facts & Statistics: Anxiety and Depression," Anxiety and Depression Association of America, <http://www.adaa.org/about-adaa/press-room/facts-statistics> (April 8, 2015).
6. Ibid.
7. Francis Mark Mondimore, *Depression, the Mood Disease* (Baltimore, Md.: Johns Hopkins University Press, 1993), p. 151.
8. "Facts & Statistics: Anxiety and Depression."
9. Ibid.
10. "Borderline Personality Disorder," National Alliance on Mental Illness, <https://www.nami.org/Learn-More/Mental-Health-Conditions/Borderline-Personality-Disorder> (April 8, 2015).
11. Mondimore, p. 165.

## Chapter 7: Getting Help

1. Anne Sheffield, *How You Can Survive When They're Depressed* (New York, N.Y.: Three Rivers Press, 1998), p. 1.

2. Rosalynn Carter and Susan K. Golant, *Helping Someone with Mental Illness* (New York, N.Y.: Three Rivers Press, 1999), p. 7.
3. Demitri F. Papolos and Janice Papolos, *Overcoming Depression* (New York, N.Y.: Harper & Row Publishers, 1987), p. 167.
4. Francis Mark Mondimore, *Depression, the Mood Disease* (Baltimore, Md.: Johns Hopkins University Press, 1993), p. 197.
5. Carter and Golant, p. 19.
6. Carol Turkington and Eliot F. Kaplan, *Making the Antidepressant Decision* (Chicago, Ill.: Contemporary Books, 2001), p. 2.
7. David A. Karp, *Speaking of Sadness: Depression, Disconnection, and the Meanings of Illness* (New York, N.Y.: Oxford University Press, 1996), p. 12.
8. Mondimore, p. 83.
9. Ibid., p. 198.
10. Aron Halfin, "Depression: The Benefits of Early and Appropriate Treatment," *The American Journal of Managed Care*, November 13, 2007, (4 Suppl): S92–7.
11. Carter and Golant, p. 3.
12. Sheffield, p. 9.
13. Carter and Golant, p. 18.
14. Ibid., p. 23.
15. Mondimore, p. 223.
16. Sheffield, p. viii.
17. "Suicide Facts," Suicide Awareness Voices of Education, <http://www.save.org/index.cfm?fuseaction=home.viewPage&page_id=705D5DF4-055B-F1EC-3F66462866FCB4E6> (April 8, 2015).
18. Sheffield, p. 233.
19. Ibid., p. 234.
20. Richard O'Connor, "Teen Suicide," Focus Adolescent Services,

n.d., <http://www.focusas.com/Suicide.html> (August 21, 2008).

21. Turkington and Kaplan, p. 40.
22. Papolos and Papolos, p. 162.
23. Ibid., p. 163.
24. Mark A. Reinecke and Michael R. Davison, eds., *Comparative Treatments of Depression* (New York, N.Y.: Springer Publishing Company, 2002), p. xiii.
25. Ginny Graves, "The Hidden Signs of Depression," *Self*, February 2007, p. 101.
26. Carter and Golant, p. 153.
27. "True Quotes About Overcoming Depression," Wordsheaven, <http://www.wordsheaven.com/overcoming-depression.html> (April 8, 2015).
28. Ibid.

# Glossary

*adrenal glands*—Two glands located near the kidneys that produce chemicals to help the body function and are thought to be involved in the human stress response.

*adversity*—Serious hardships and troubles.

*affective*—Having to do with emotions and feelings.

*anti-inflammatory*—Something that works against irritation or inflammation in the body.

*avoidance*—A psychological term for behavior that involves staying away from or avoiding things that are upsetting.

*clinical depression*—A name for depression as a disease or illness.

*dopamine*—A neurotransmitter that may play a role in feelings of reward or pleasure.

*dysfunctional*—Behavior or situations that result in negative consequences or feelings; something that does not contribute to positive functioning.

*dysthymia*—A chronic or ongoing form of depression; may not be as severe as major depression but lasts longer.

*electroconvulsive treatment (ECT, also known as electroshock therapy)*—The use of an electric current to stimulate the brain as a treatment for depression and other mental disorders.

*enzyme*—A substance that causes a particular chemical reaction to occur.

*euphoria*—An extreme feeling of happiness and well-being.

*generic*—Not trademarked.

*genetics*—Having to do with heredity or the origins of something.

*hormones*—Chemicals released into the bloodstream by a number of glands in the body that influence body functions and behavior.

*hypothalamus*—A part of the brain that connects the brain with various systems in the body.

*limbic region*—A part of the brain thought to be involved with emotions and behavior.

*major depressive disorder (MDD)*—The term for depressive disorder used in the *Diagnostic and Statistical Manual of Mental Disorders* (*DSM*). A number of symptoms need to be present to be diagnosed with MDD.

*mania*—An extremely intense or exaggerated enthusiasm or excitement.

*mastery*—In psychological terms, having a sense of being in control of or able to deal with a situation.

*melancholy*—A term used since ancient times for illnesses that include physical and emotional symptoms.

*monoamines*—A group of chemicals in the body that includes neurotransmitters.

*neuron*—A nerve cell.

*neurotransmitter*—A chemical that acts as a messenger between neurons.

*norepinephrine*—A neurotransmitter thought to play a role in attention and response.

*phobia*—An extreme fear that is usually of something not everyone is afraid of.

# Glossary

*pituitary gland*—A small gland at the bottom of the brain that sends messages to other glands and plays a role in a number of body functions.

*placebo*—A substitute for real medicine in a research study; a harmless but ineffective pill given in place of real medicine to compare with the effects of the real medicine. Sometimes called a sugar pill.

*psychiatry*—A branch of medicine specializing in the study of mental illness.

*psychoanalysis*—Form of psychotherapy developed by Sigmund Freud.

*psychotherapy*—Treatments that use psychology and psychological research in the treatment of mental illness.

*reuptake*—The absorption or elimination of a substance.

*serotonin*—A neurotransmitter thought to play an important role in mood.

*steroid*—A type of medication used in many ways that is not to be confused with anabolic steroids, which are used illegally as performance-enhancing drugs by some athletes.

*stigma*—A negative meaning or attitude attached to something.

*syndrome*—A group of symptoms that occur together.

*thyroid gland*—A gland found in the neck that plays a role in energy levels.

*tyramine*—A substance found in some foods that can cause blood pressure to rise dangerously.

**unipolar depression (or unipolar disorder)**—Depression without the extreme highs, or mania, of bipolar depression.

# For More Information

**National Suicide Prevention Lifeline**
1-800-273-TALK (8255)

**Anxiety and Depression Association of America**
8701 Georgia Ave., Suite #412
Silver Spring, MD 20910
240-485-1001
adaa.org

**Depression and Bipolar Support Alliance (DBSA)**
55 East Jackson Blvd., Suite 490
Chicago, IL 60604
1-800-826-3632
dbsalliance.org

**International Foundation for Research and Education on Depression (iFred)**
820 West Jackson, Suite 805
Chicago, IL 60607
info@ifred.org
ifred.org

**National Alliance on Mental Illness (NAMI)**
3803 N. Fairfax Drive
Arlington VA 22203
HelpLine: 800-950-NAMI (6264)
Monday–Friday, 10 am to 6 pm Eastern Standard Time
703-524-7600

# Further Reading

Cantopher, Tim. *Depressive Illness: The Curse of the Strong*. The London, England: Society for Promoting Christian Knowledge, 2012.

Forney, Ellen. Marbles: *Mania, Depression, Michelangelo, and Me: A Graphic Memoir.* New York, N.Y.: Avery, 2012.

Goldstein, Elisha. *Uncovering Happiness: Overcoming Depression with Mindfulness and Self-Compassion.* New York, N.Y.: Atria/Simon & Schuster, 2015.

Ilardi, Stephen. *The Depression Cure: The 6-Step Program to Beat Depression without Drugs.* Boston, Mass.: Da Capo Lifelong Books, 2010

Kirsch, Irving. *The Emperor's New Drugs: Exploding the Antidepressant Myth.* New York, N.Y.: Basic Books, 2011.

O'Connor, Richard. *Undoing Depression: What Therapy Doesn't Teach You and Medication Can't Give You.* Boston, Mass.: Little Brown and Company, 2010.

Rice-Oxley, Mark. *Underneath the Lemon Tree: A Memoir of Depression and Recovery*. Boston, Mass.: Little Brown and Company, 2012.

Smith, Daniel. *Monkey Mind: A Memoir of Anxiety*. New York, N.Y.: Simon & Schuster, 2013.

Teasdale, John and Mark Williams. *The Mindful Way Workbook; An 8-Week Program to Free Yourself from Depression and Emotional Distress.* New York, N.Y.: The Guildford Press, 2014.

Tompkins, Michael. *My Anxious Mind: A Teen's Guide to Managing Anxiety and Panic.* Washington, D.C.: Magination Press, 2009.

*Are You Depressed?*

## Web Sites

**aacap.org**

The American Academy of Child and Adolescent Psychiatry Web site provides facts, resource centers, research, and a psychiatrist finder.

**depressionconnection.org**

Depression Connection has information about depression, bipolar disorder, and anxiety, including resources on how to get help.

**save.org**

SAVE: Suicide Awareness Voices of Education develops programs to educate the public about clinical depression and suicide prevention.

**studentsagainstdepresssion.org**

Students Against Depression features information and resources from health professionals as well as advice from students who have suffered from depression firsthand.

# Index

## A
abuse, 30, 41
active listening, 72
anticonvulsants, 86
antidepressants, 9, 16, 18, 36, 52, 54–58, 60–61, 64–65, 67, 69, 75–78, 86–87, 89, 91, 100
antipsychotics, 18, 86–87
anxiety disorders, 43, 83, 87–89, 91
avoidance, 42–43, 89

## B
Beck, Aaron, 73
behavioral rehearsal, 72
behavior therapy, 72–73, 75
bipolar disorder, 10, 24, 81, 83–84, 86–87, 91
borderline personality disorder (BPD), 91
bright light therapy, 78

## C
Carter, Rosalynn, 97–98, 105
causes of depression
  brain disorders, physical, 10, 16, 34, 36–37, 39
  genetic, 38–39, 84
  hormonal, 30, 37–38, 47
  illness-related, 22, 47–48
  medications, 36, 48–49, 52, 100
  neurotransmitters, 34, 52, 54–55, 62
  psychological, 10, 16, 34, 39, 69, 70–71, 96
  sleep disorders, 44
Celexa (citalopram), 58
chemical dependency, 91–92
children, depression in, 29–30, 44, 47, 57, 86
chlorpromazine (Thorazine), 18
Churchill, Winston, 10
cognitive therapy, 73, 75–76
coping skills, 39, 41–42, 44, 69, 71–72, 76, 87, 94
counseling, 69–71, 98

## D
Depakote (valproic acid), 87
depression
  causes. *See causes of depression.*
  people affected by, 8, 29, 84, 89, 93
  symptoms. *See symptoms of depression.*
  treatment. *See treatment.*
diagnosis
  factors affecting, 22, 24–25, 29, 45
  process, 22–24

professionals qualified for, 22–23
*Diagnostic and Statistical Manual of Mental Disorders (DSM)*, 19, 24–25, 87
discrimination, 97–98
distorted thinking, 42, 44, 100
dopamine, 36–37, 54, 62, 64
Duke, Patty, 86, 107
dysthymia, 24–25

# E
Effexor (venlafaxine), 64
elderly adults, 32
electroshock therapy, 16, 60, 77
Ellis, Albert, 73
exercise, 14, 51, 78, 107

# F
family effects, 69, 77, 94, 98
Franklin, Benjamin, 14
Freud, Sigmund, 16, 60, 72

# G
generalized anxiety disorder (GAD), 89
genetic causes, 38–39, 84
group therapy, 77

# H
hepatitis, 48
Hippocrates, 11, 65
hospitalization, 47, 78, 84, 98, 100
Huntington's disease, 48
hypericin, 65
hypothyroidism, 47

# I
imipramine (Tofranil), 18, 60–61
infections, 48
insurance, 81, 98, 105
interpersonal therapy (IPT), 76

# L
Lincoln, Abraham, 11
lithium, 86–87
Luvox (fluvoxamine), 58

# M
magnetic stimulation, 78, 80
mastery, 41
medical history, 24, 33, 38–39
medications. *See also specific medications.*
  adverse reactions to, 58
  antidepressants. 9, 16, 18, 36, 52, 54–58, 60–61, 64–65, 67, 69, 75–78, 86–87, 89, 91, 100
  bipolar disorder, 86–87
  brand name vs. generic, 54
  development, history of, 16, 18, 52, 54, 57, 61–62, 70, 107
  herbal, 65
  MAOIs, 54, 61–63
  neurotransmitter deficiency, 36, 52, 54, 57, 61–62, 65, 77–78
  psychotherapy vs., 70, 76, 80
  research, 18, 57, 60, 65, 70, 89

# Index

side effects, 52, 56–58, 61–65, 70, 76, 78, 80, 107
   for sleep, 48, 64–65
   SSRIs, 54, 58, 60–61, 65
   suicide and, 100
   tricyclics, 54, 60–61, 91
melancholy, 11, 14, 86
Mendel, Gregor, 38
monoamine hypothesis, 36
mood disorders, 8, 11, 24, 38–39, 73, 92, 96, 107
multiple sclerosis, 22, 48

## N
National Alliance for the Mentally Ill (NAMI), 105
National Depressive and Manic Depressive Association (NDMDA), 104–105
negative thinking, 10, 21, 42, 44, 69, 73, 75, 100
neurotransmitters, 34, 36–37, 52, 54–58, 61–62, 64–65, 77–78
norepinephrine, 36–37, 54, 61–62, 64, 91

## O
obsessive-compulsive disorder (OCD), 58, 88

## P
panic disorder, 58, 87–88
Parkinson's disease, 22, 48
Pauley, Jane, 107
Paxil (paroxetine), 18, 58
phobias, 29, 43, 58, 88

physician/general practitioners, 14, 22, 52, 61
postpartum depression/psychosis, 30
posttraumatic stress disorder (PTSD), 58, 64, 89
pregnancy, 30, 57
Prozac (fluoxetine), 18, 58
psychiatrists, 16, 19, 22–24, 51–52, 60–61, 63, 70, 86, 94, 98
psychoanalysis, 16, 60, 72
psychodynamic therapy, 77
psychologists, 18, 24, 29, 45, 51, 70, 73
psychotherapy, 70–73, 76, 80–81, 89, 91

## R
recurrence rates, 33
relabeling, 73
relaxation training, 72
Rogers, Carl, 72
Rush, Benjamin, 15

## S
schizophrenia, 16, 18, 60
seasonal affective disorder (SAD), 45, 78
self-esteem, 41, 69
self-help, 104
serotonin, 36–37, 54, 58, 61–62, 64, 91
sleep disorders, 44, 67
sleep medications, 48, 64–65
social anxiety disorder, 88
St. John's wort, 65, 67

steroids, 48–49
stigma, 8, 97–98
substance abuse, 24, 30
suicide
   adolescents and teens, 29, 99–101
   antidepressants and, 100
   preventive measures, 103
   risk factors, 84, 100–101
   warning signs, 100–101
support, 41, 70, 94, 96, 104
symptoms of depression
   behavioral, 10, 21, 29–30, 32, 42–43, 69–71, 81, 84, 89
   cognitive, 21
   *DSM* listing, 25
   emotional, 10–11, 20–21, 26, 34, 86, 89, 91
   physical, 10–11, 14, 20–21, 26, 30, 34, 70, 87, 91, 96

# T

teens, depression in, 8, 29–30, 44, 86, 99–101
Tegretol (carbamazepine), 87
thinking disorders
   distorted, 42, 44, 100
   negativity, 10, 21, 42, 44, 69, 73, 75, 100

thioridazine, 86
thyroid deficiency, 22, 38, 47
treatment
   active listening, 72
   behavior therapy, 72–73, 75
   bright light, 78
   cognitive therapy, 73, 75–76
   counseling, 69–71, 98
   electroshock therapy, 16, 60, 77
   exercise, 14, 51, 78, 107
   group therapy, 77
   hospitalization, 47, 78, 84, 98, 100
   interpersonal therapy, 76
   magnetic stimulation, 78, 80
   medications. *See medications.*
   psychodynamic therapy, 77
   resources, 105
   self-help, 104
   support, 41, 70, 94, 96, 104
tyramine, 62

# W

Wallace, Mike, 98
Wellbutrin (bupropion), 64

# Z

Zoloft (sertraline), 18, 58